Dear parents, caregivers, and educators:

If you want to get your child excited about reading, you've come to the right place! Ready-to-Read *GRAPHICS* is the perfect launchpad for emerging graphic novel readers.

All Ready-to-Read *GRAPHICS* books include the following:

- ★ **A how-to guide to reading graphic novels for first-time readers**

- ★ **Easy-to-follow panels to support reading comprehension**

- ★ **Accessible vocabulary to build your child's reading confidence**

- ★ **Compelling stories that star your child's favorite characters**

- ★ **Fresh, engaging illustrations that provide context and promote visual literacy**

Wherever your child may be on their reading journey, Ready-to-Read *GRAPHICS* will make them giggle, gasp, and want to keep reading more.

Blast off on this starry adventure . . . a universe of graphic novel reading awaits!

THUNDER AND CLUCK

The **Brave Friend** Leads the Way!

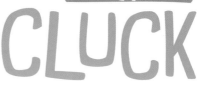

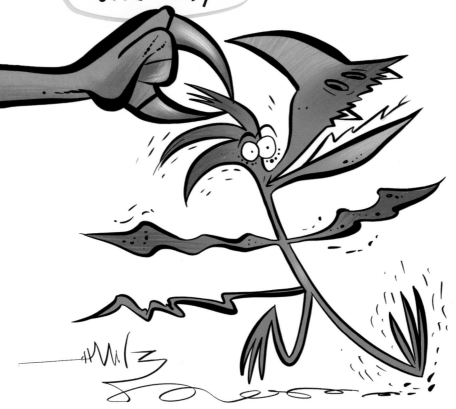

For Bennett & Lawson
—J. E.

With Love for My Old Man,
who gave me the Sea.
Thank you, Dad.
—M. T.

SIMON SPOTLIGHT
An imprint of Simon & Schuster Children's Publishing Division
1230 Avenue of the Americas, New York, New York 10020
This Simon Spotlight edition August 2021
Text copyright © 2021 by Jill Esbaum
Illustrations copyright © 2021 by Christopher M. Thompson
All rights reserved, including the right of reproduction in whole or in part in any form.
SIMON SPOTLIGHT, READY-TO-READ, and colophon are registered trademarks
of Simon & Schuster, Inc. For information about special discounts for bulk
purchases, please contact Simon & Schuster Special Sales at 1-866-506-1949 or
business@simonandschuster.com.
Manufactured in the United States of America 0721 LAK
10 9 8 7 6 5 4 3 2 1
Library of Congress Cataloging-in-Publication Data
Names: Esbaum, Jill, author. | Thompson, Miles (Illustrator), illustrator. | Title: The brave
friend leads the way! / by Jill Esbaum; illustrated by Miles Thompson. | Description: Simon
Spotlight edition. | New York: Simon Spotlight, 2021. | Series: Thunder and Cluck; #2
| Summary: On a hot day, two unlikely dinosaur friends find a dark, cool cave, but who
is brave enough to lead the way in? | Identifiers: LCCN 2021003369 (print) | LCCN
2021003370 (ebook) | ISBN 9781534486553 (hardcover) | ISBN 9781534486546
(paperback) | ISBN 9781534486560 (ebook) | Subjects: LCSH: Graphic novels. | CYAC:
Graphic novels. | Dinosaurs—Fiction. | Courage—Fiction. | Friendship—Fiction. | Humorous
stories. | Classification: LCC PZ7.7.E78 Br 2021 (print) | LCC PZ7.7.E78 (ebook) | DDC
741.5/973—dc23 | LC record available at https://lccn.loc.gov/2021003369 | LC ebook
record available at https://lccn.loc.gov/2021003370

THUNDER AND CLUCK

The Brave Friend Leads the Way!

Written by **JILL ESBAUM**
Illustrated by **MILES THOMPSON**

Ready-to-Read *GRAPHICS*

Simon Spotlight
New York London Toronto Sydney New Delhi

HOW TO READ THIS BOOK

THUNDER and CLUCK are here to give you some tips on reading this book.

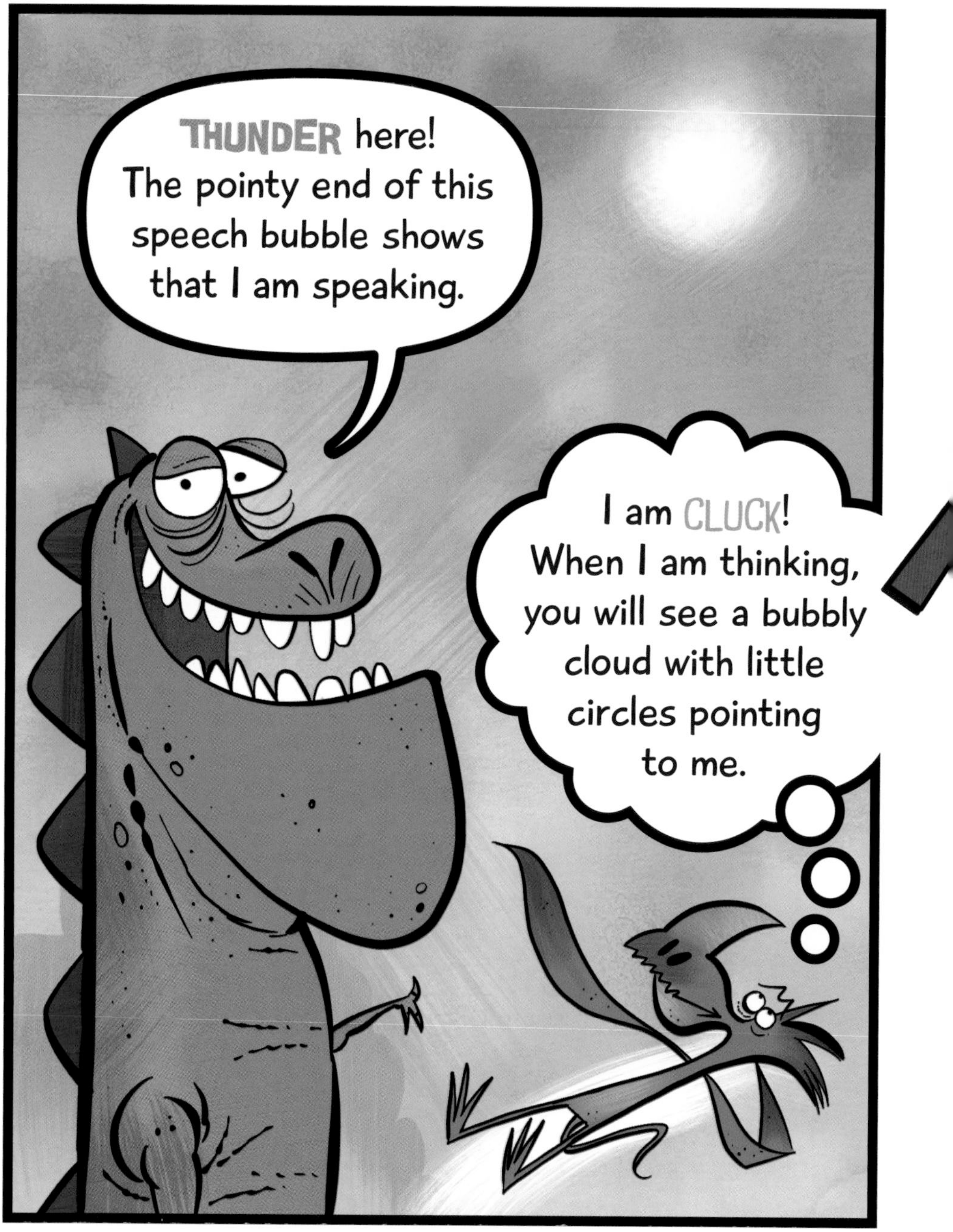
THUNDER here! The pointy end of this speech bubble shows that I am speaking.
I am CLUCK! When I am thinking, you will see a bubbly cloud with little circles pointing to me.

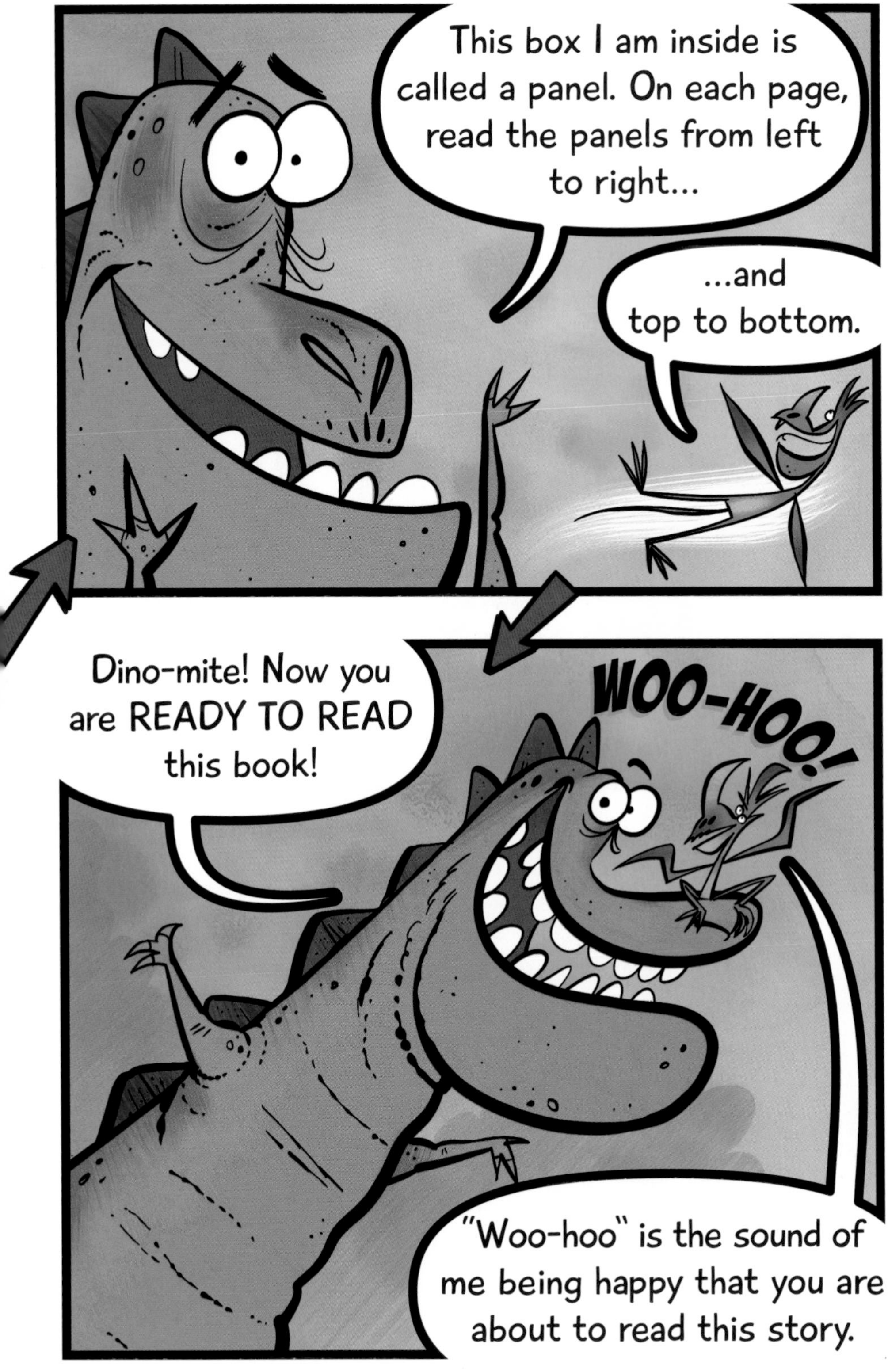
This box I am inside is called a panel. On each page, read the panels from left to right...
...and top to bottom.
Dino-mite! Now you are READY TO READ this book!
WOO-HOO!
"Woo-hoo" is the sound of me being happy that you are about to read this story.

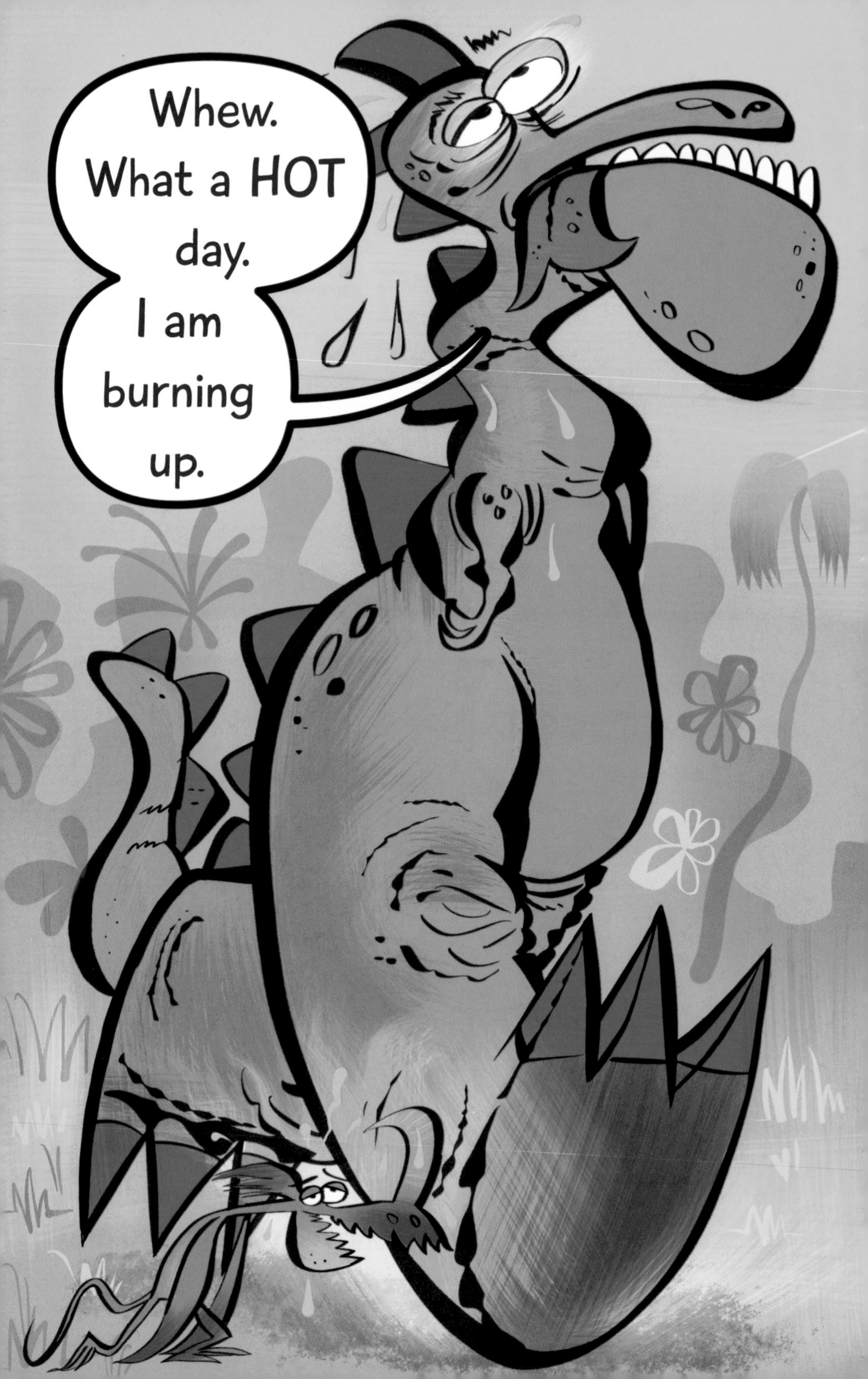
Whew. What a HOT day. I am burning up.

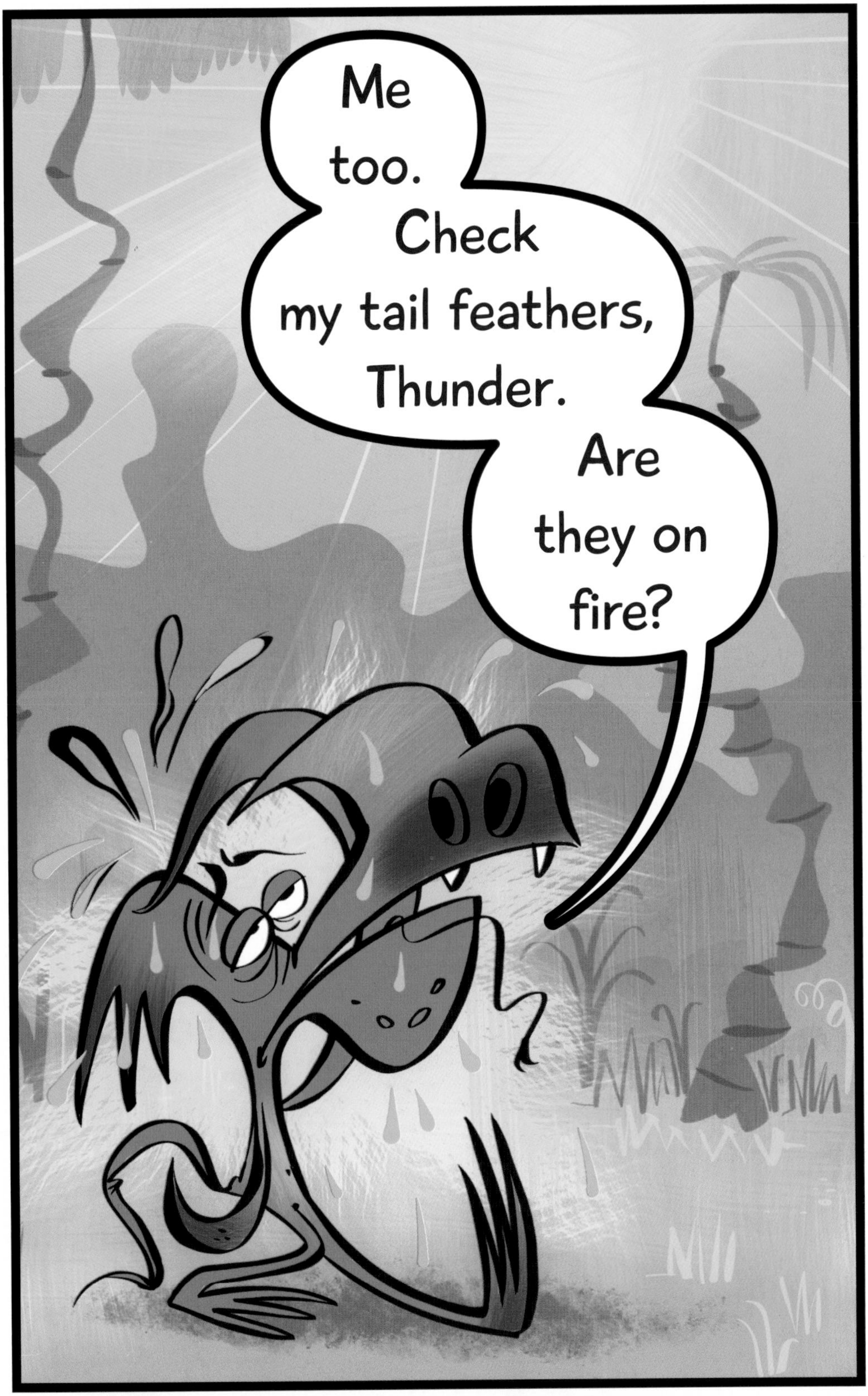
Me too. Check my tail feathers, Thunder. Are they on fire?

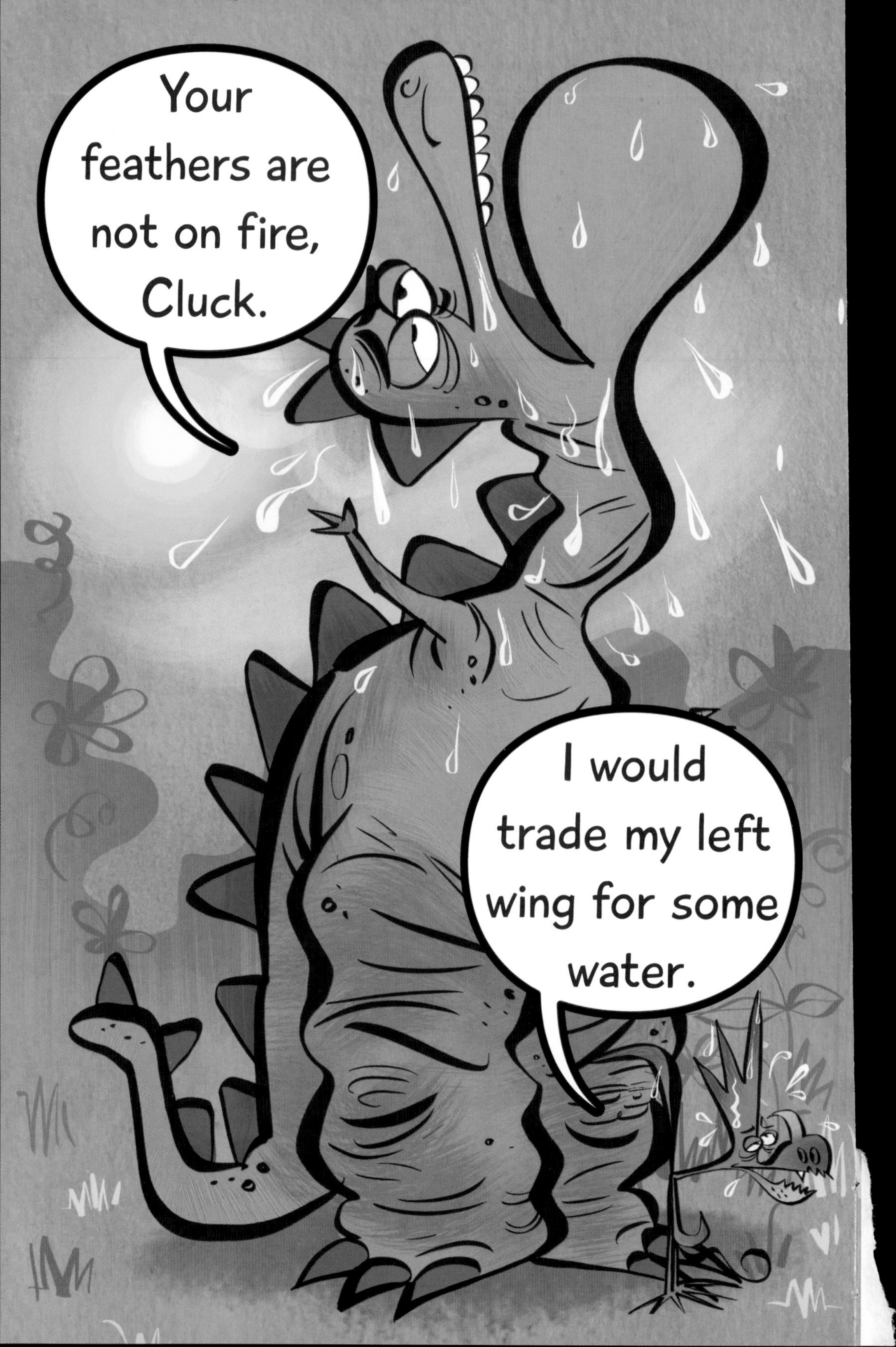
Your feathers are not on fire, Cluck.
I would trade my left wing for some water.

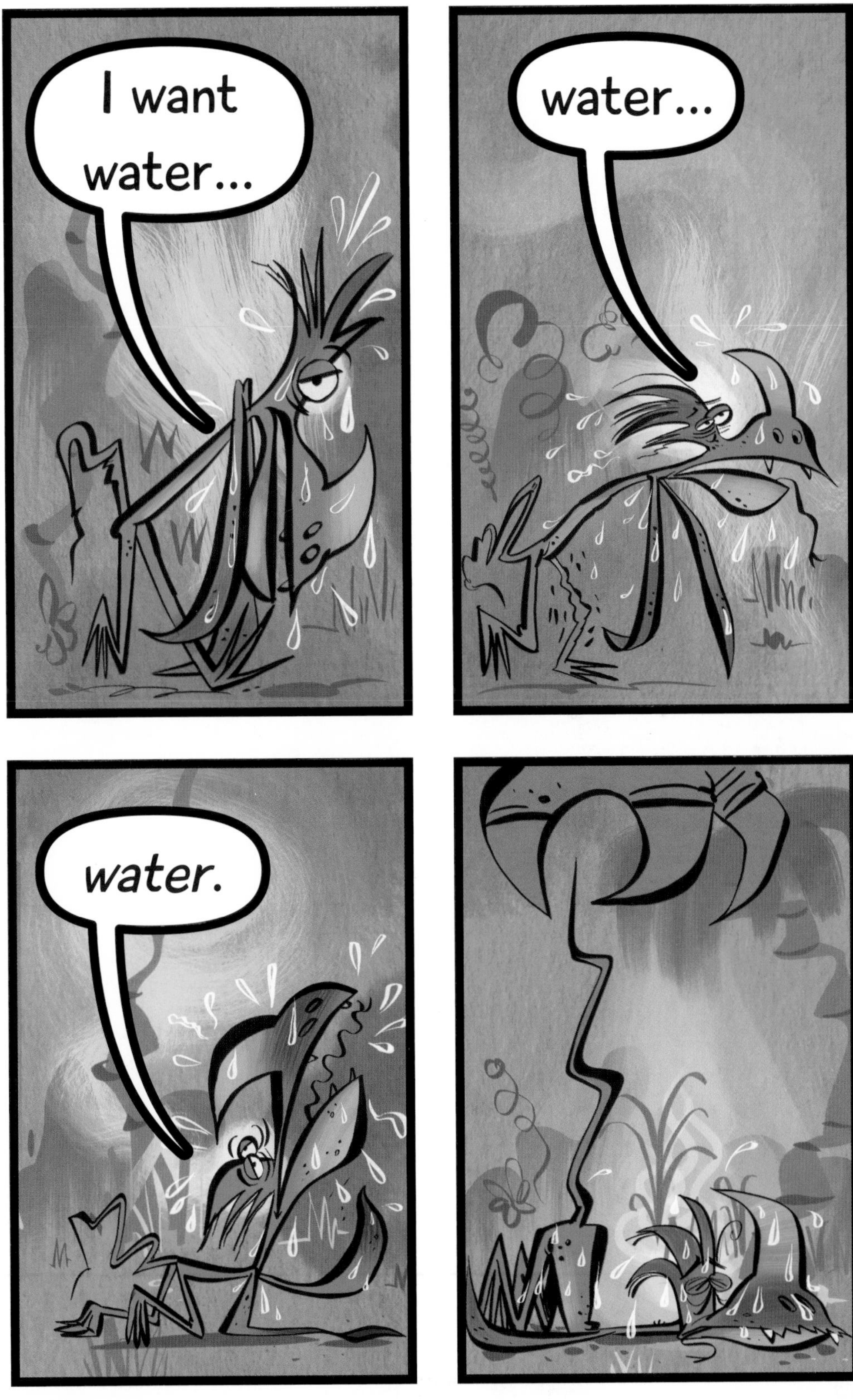
I want water...
water...
water.

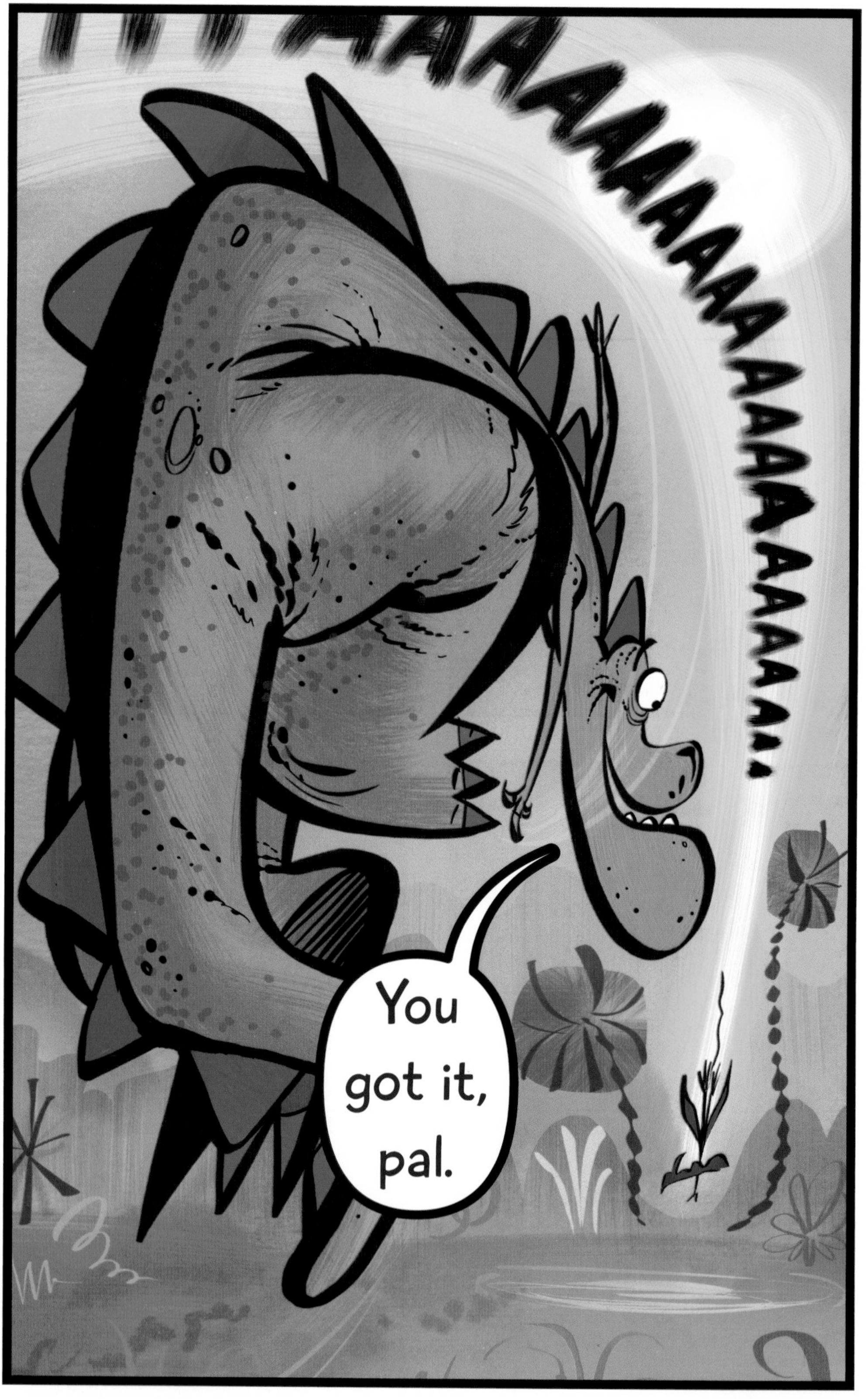
You got it, pal.

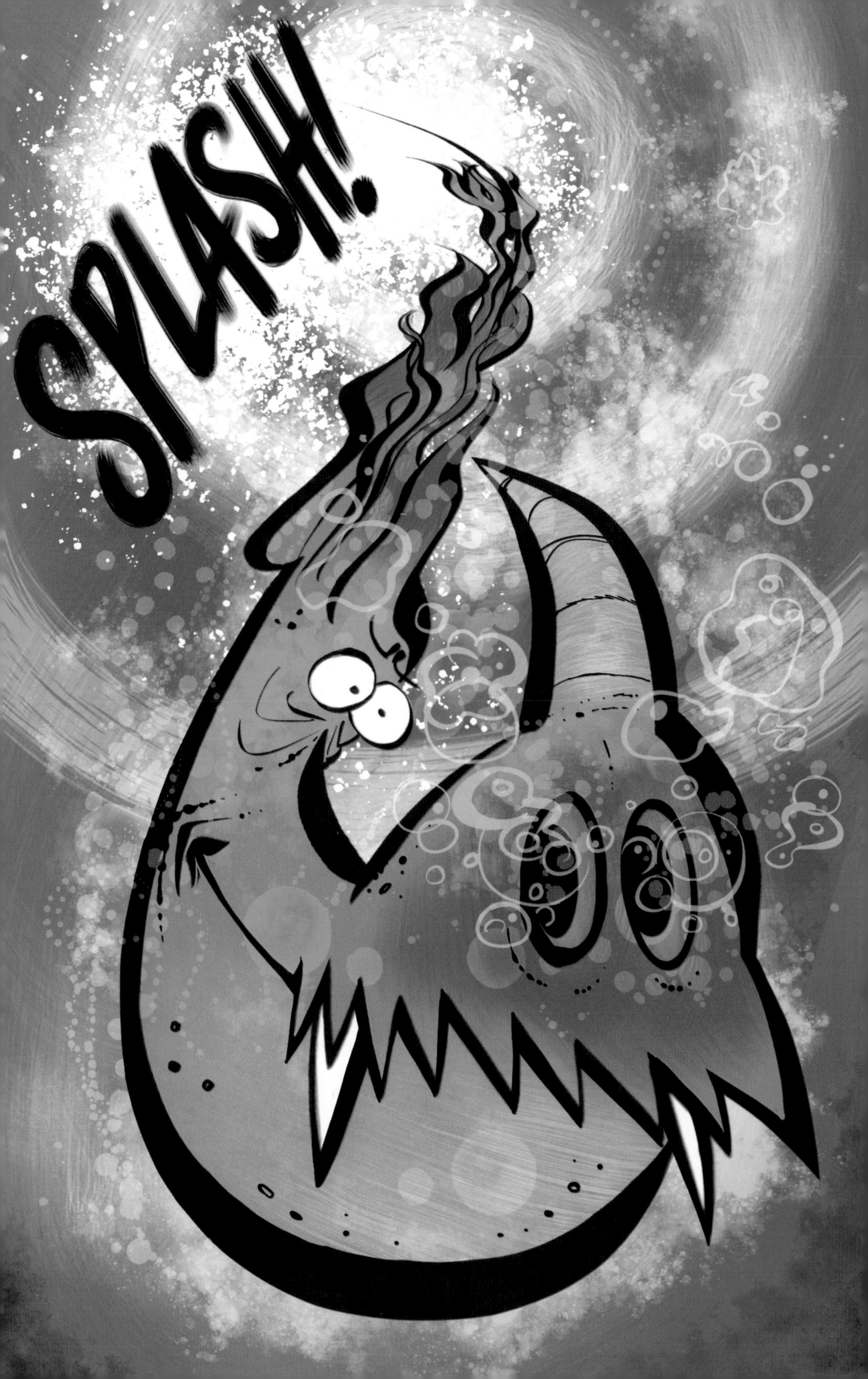
SPLASH!

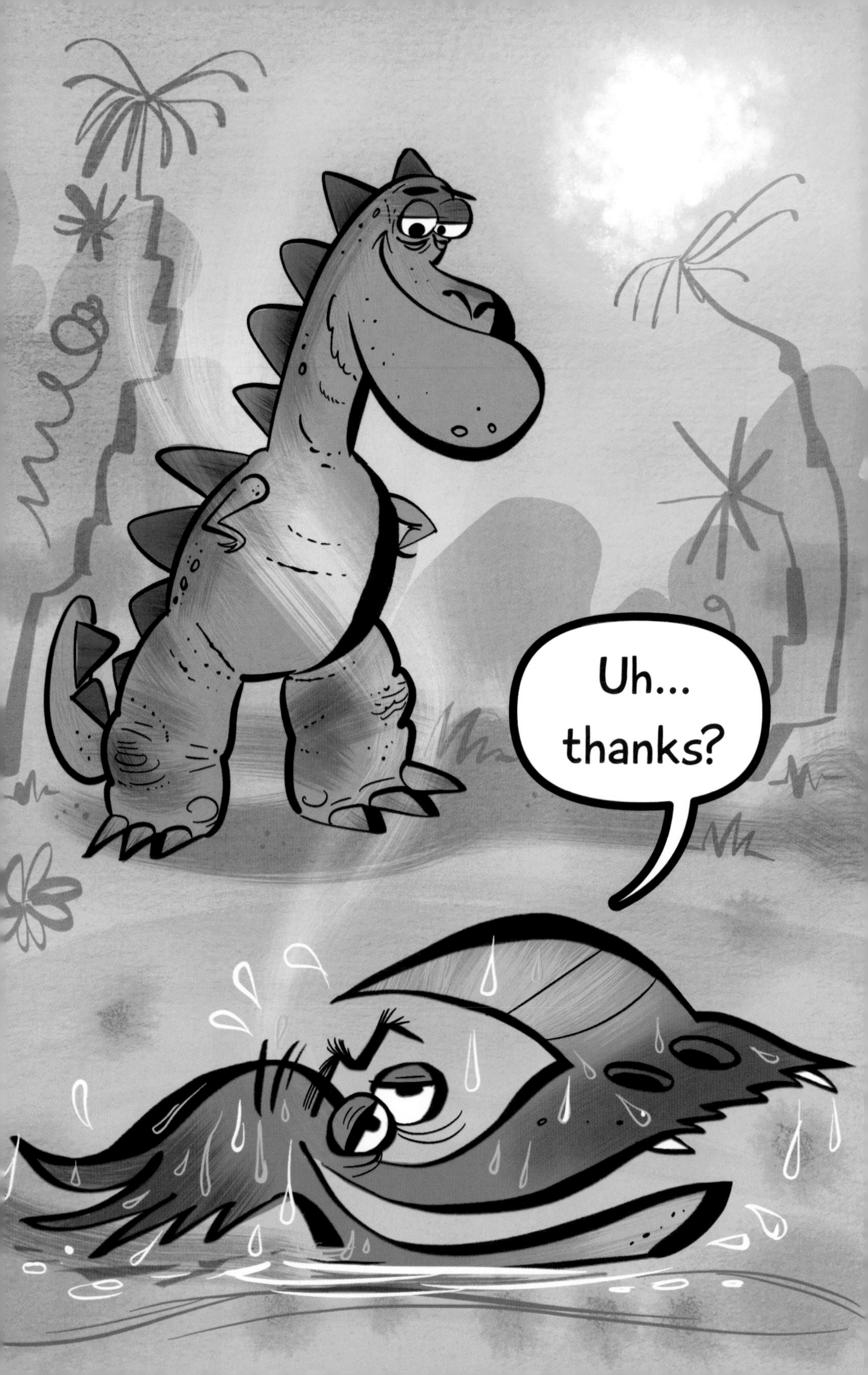
Uh... thanks?

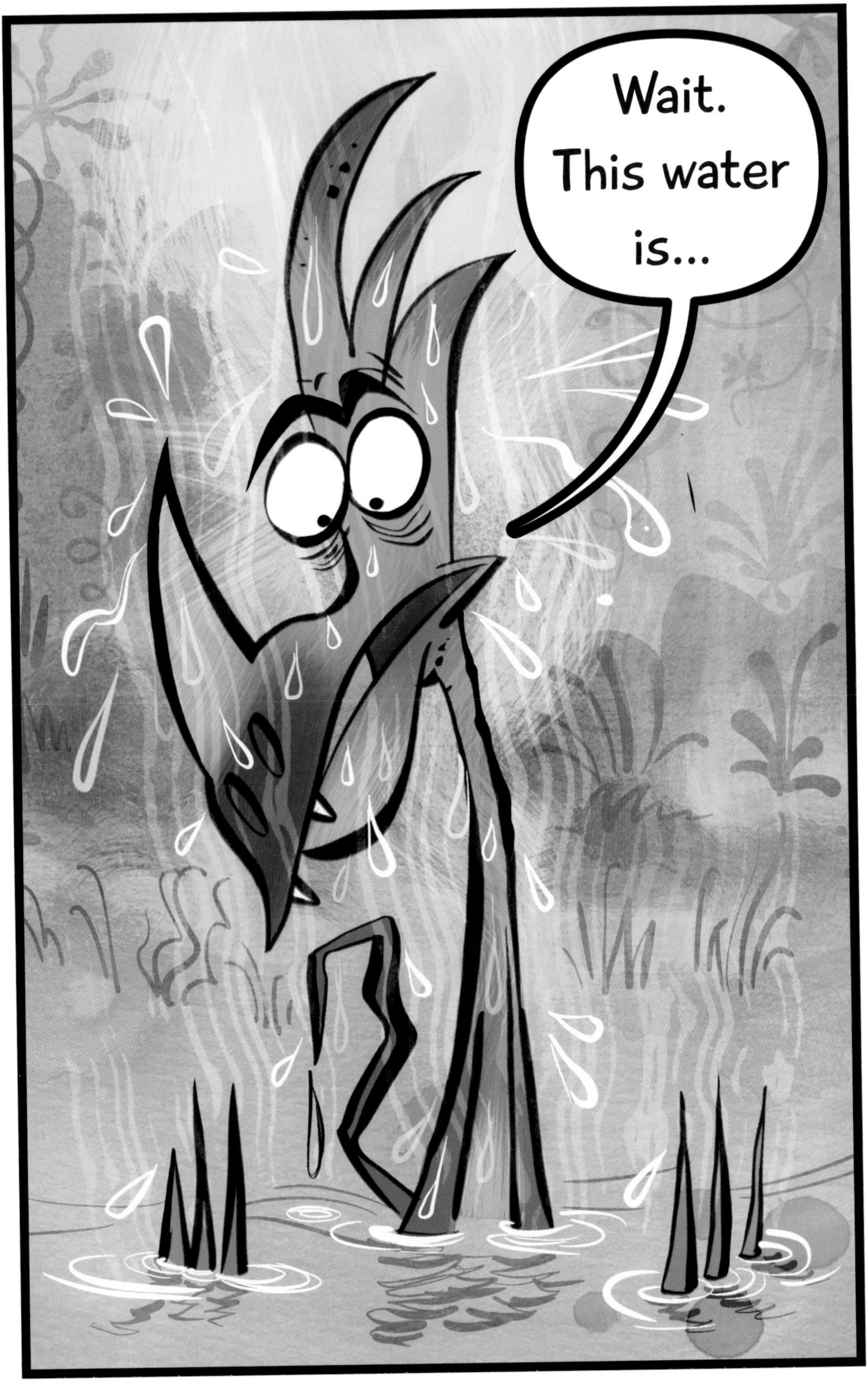
Wait. This water is...

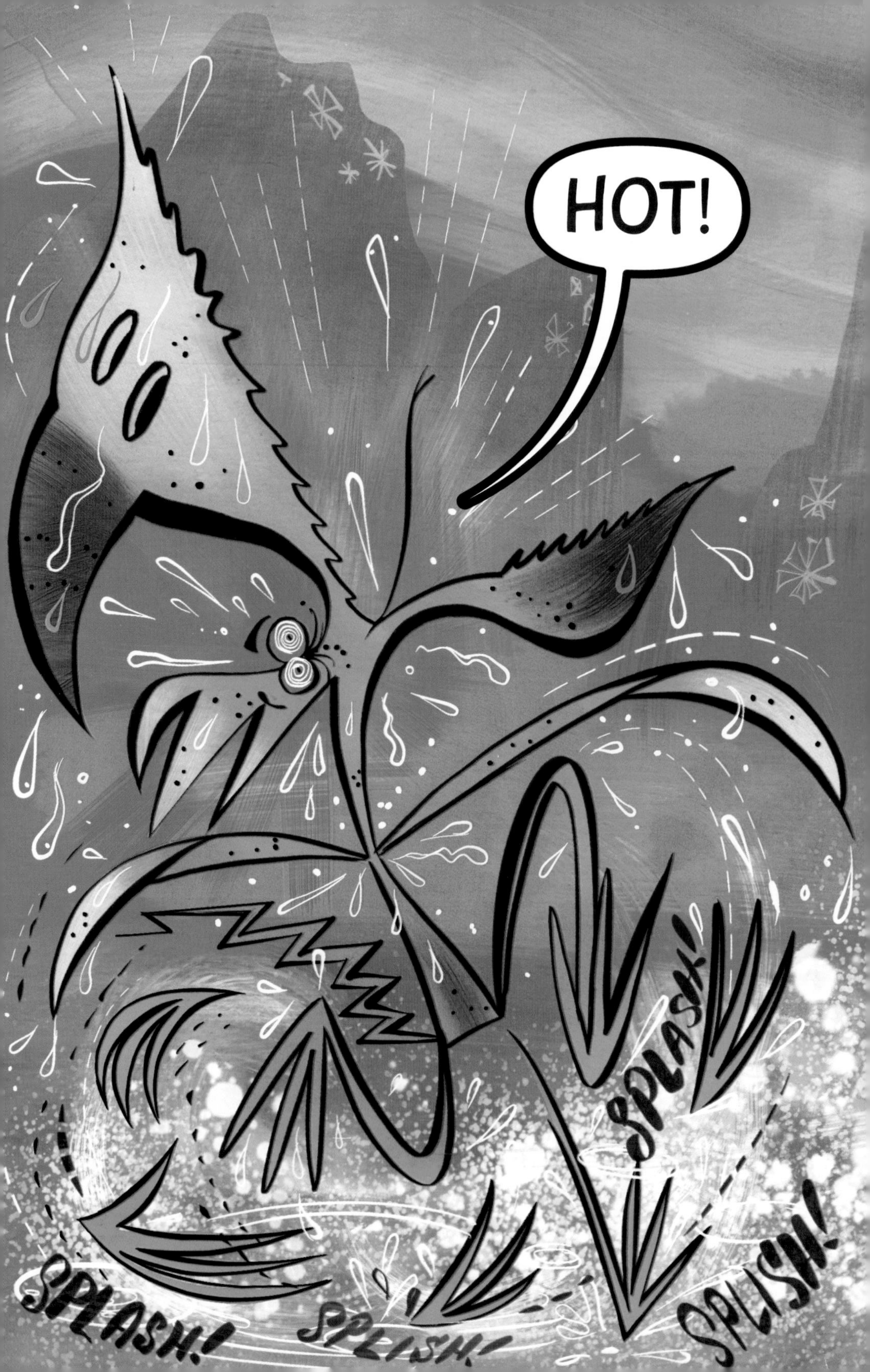
HOT!
SPLASH!
SPLASH!
SPLISH!
SPLISH!

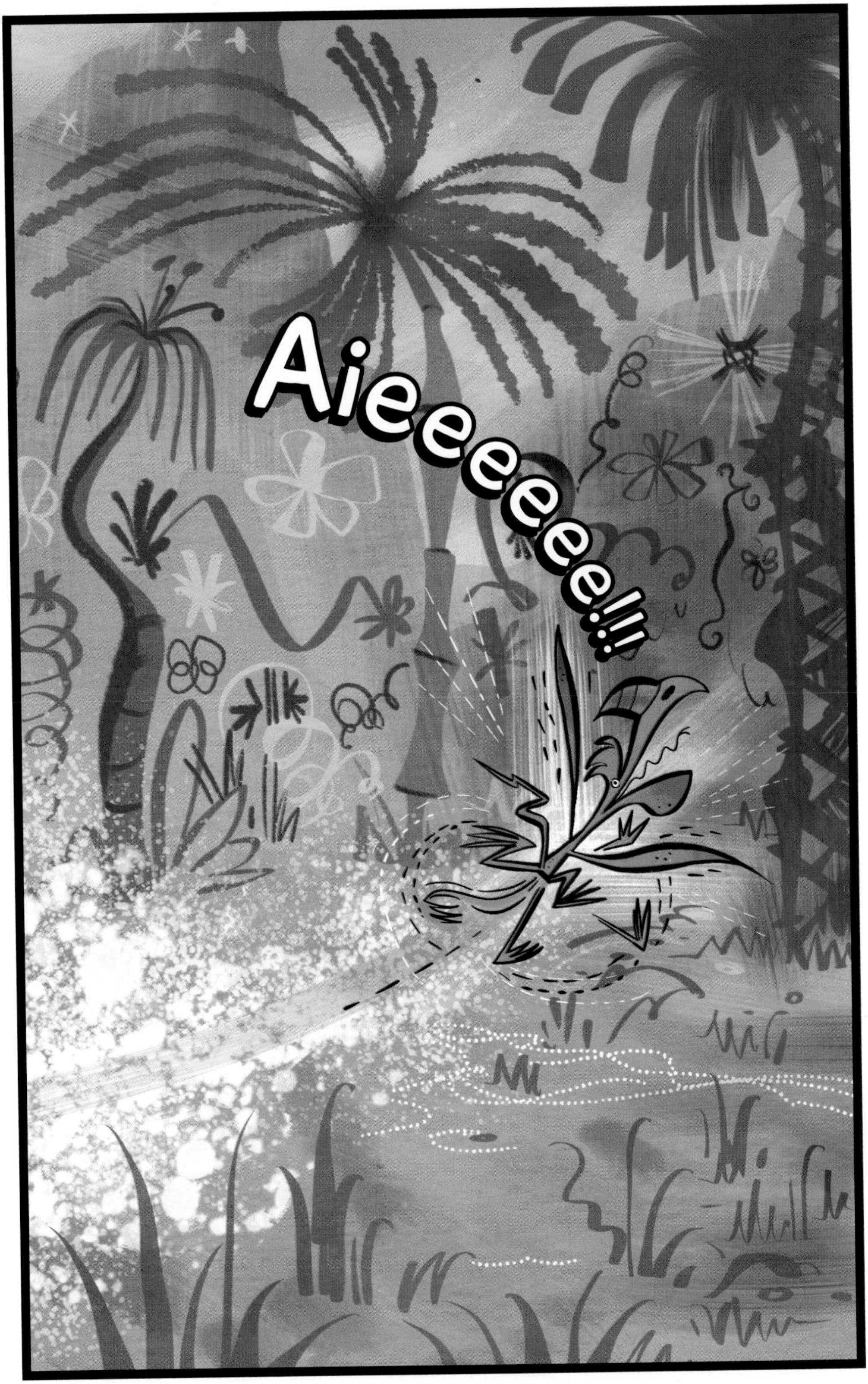
Aieeeeeee!!!

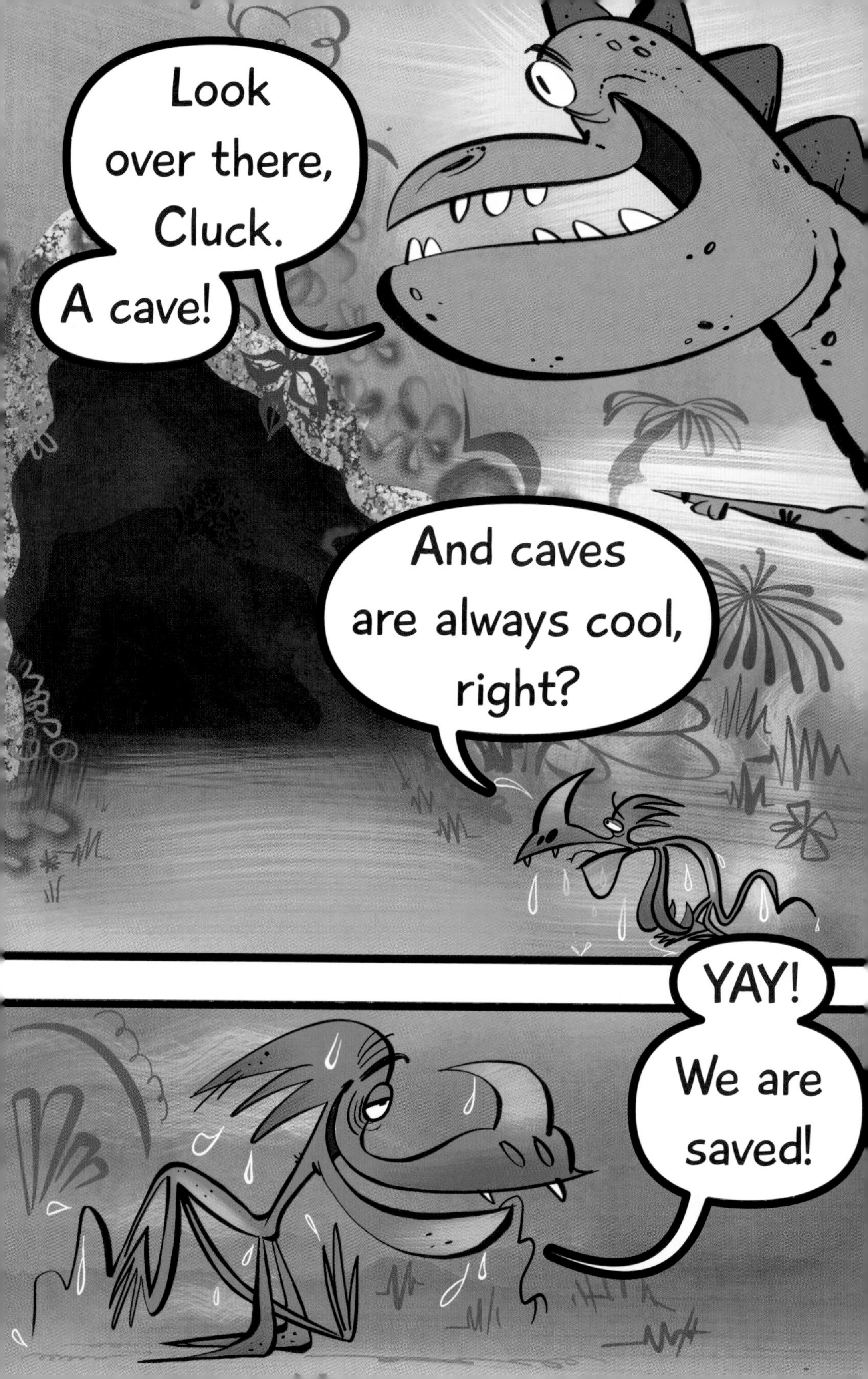
Look over there, Cluck.
A cave!
And caves are always cool, right?
YAY!
We are saved!

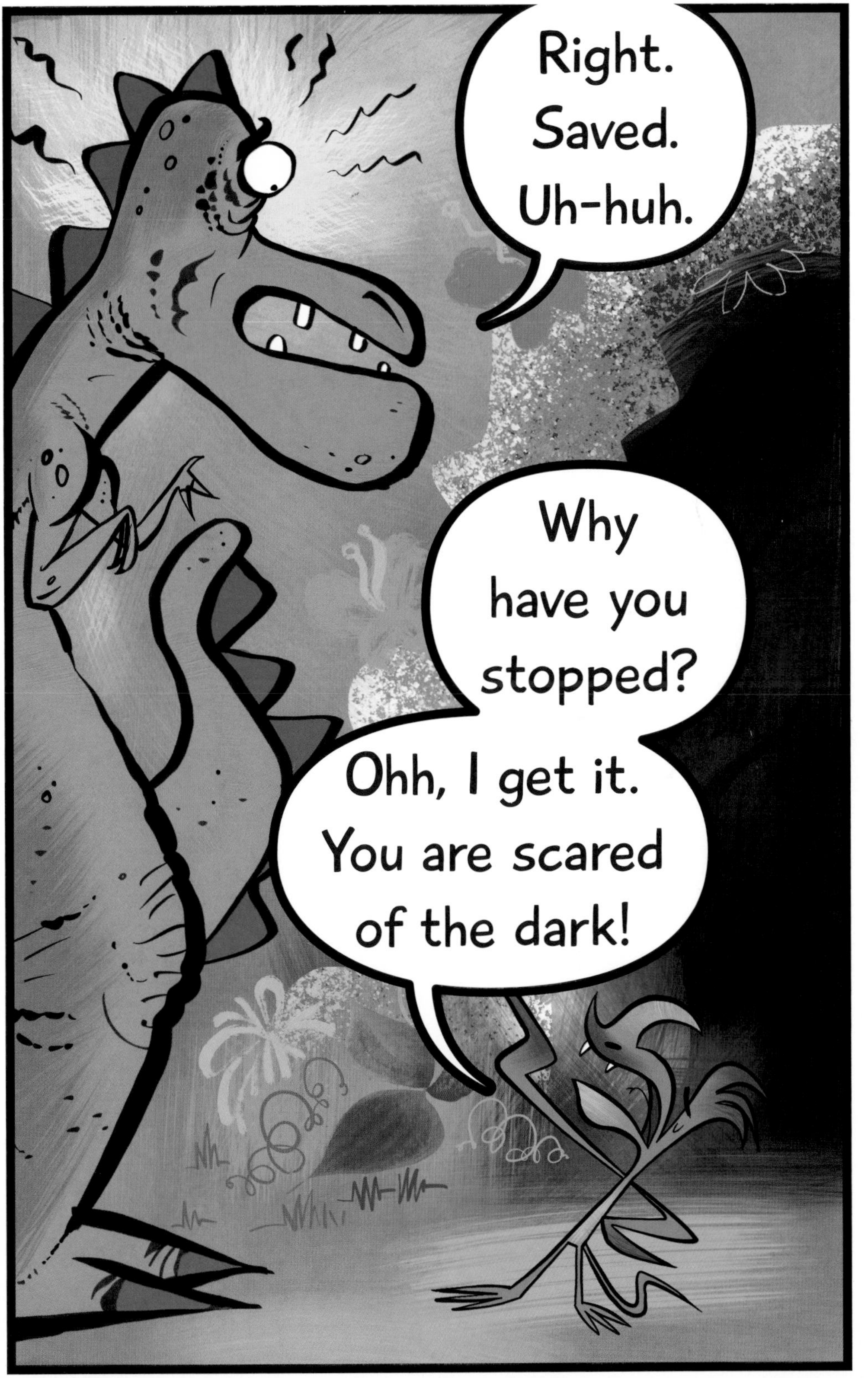
Right. Saved. Uh-huh.
Why have you stopped?
Ohh, I get it. You are scared of the dark!

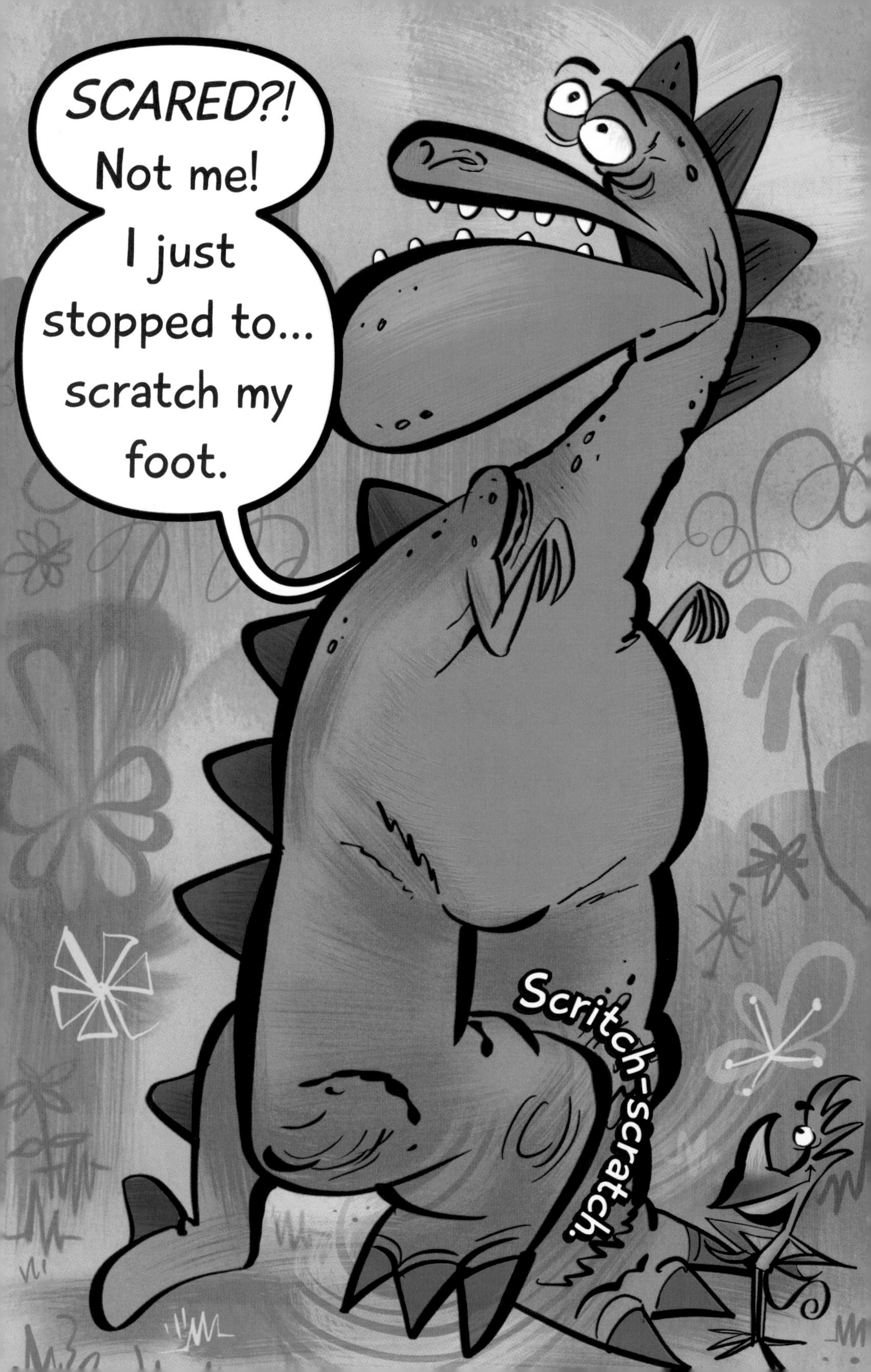
SCARED?! Not me! I just stopped to... scratch my foot.
Scritch-scratch.

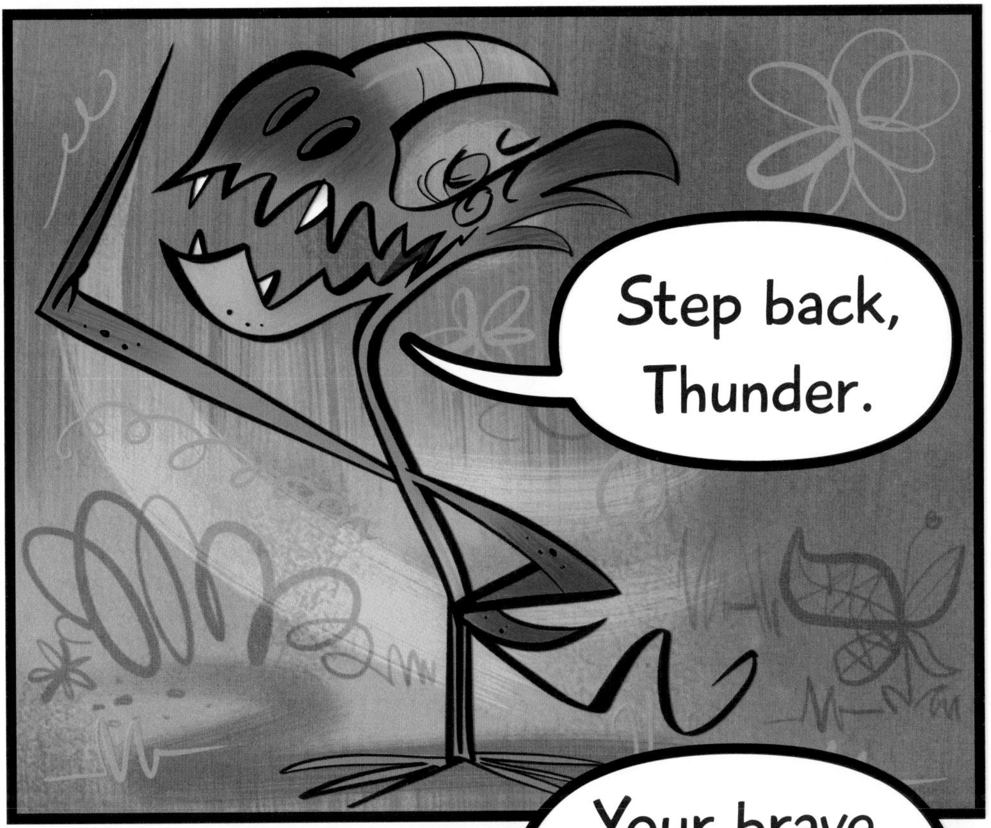
Step back, Thunder.

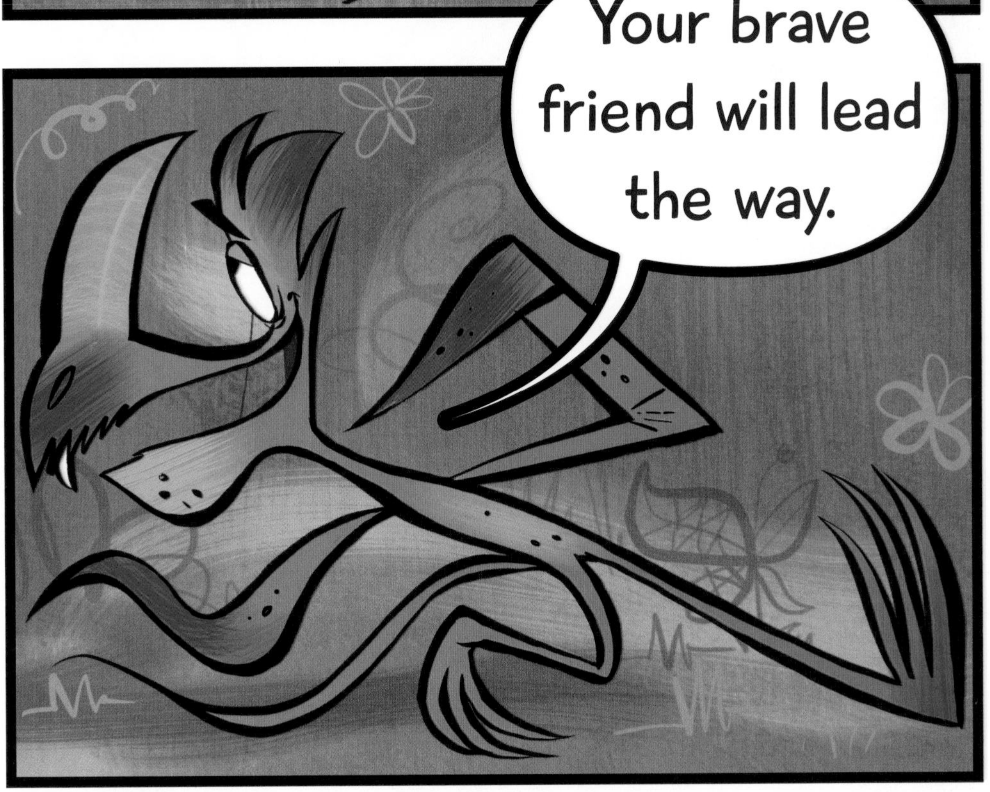
Your brave friend will lead the way.

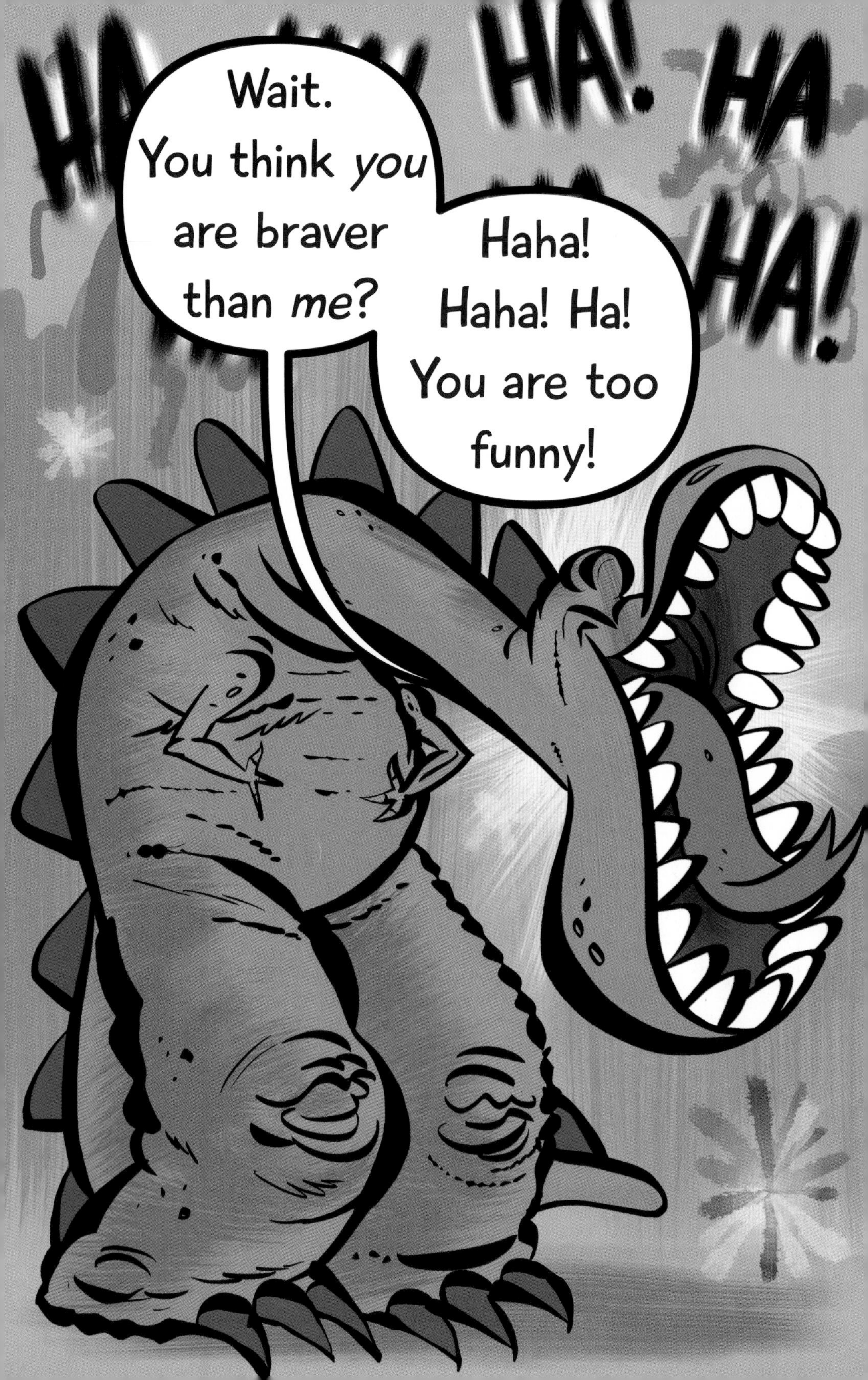
Wait.
You think *you* are braver than *me*?
Haha!
Haha! Ha!
You are too funny!
HA! HA!
HA!

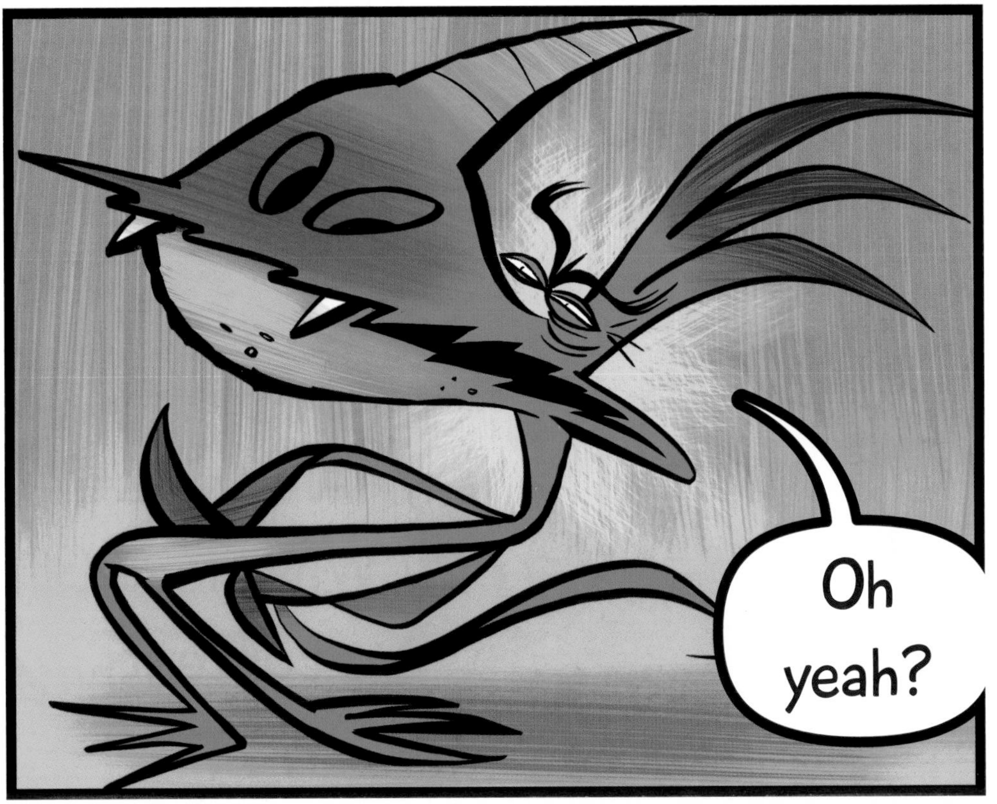
Oh yeah?

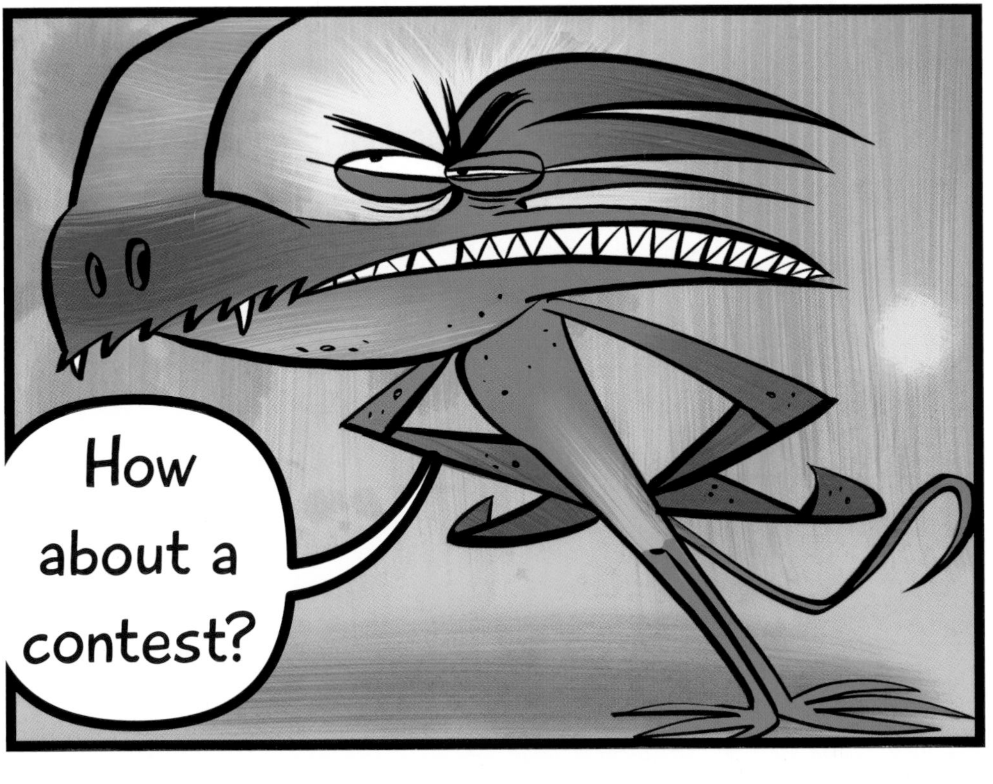
How about a contest?

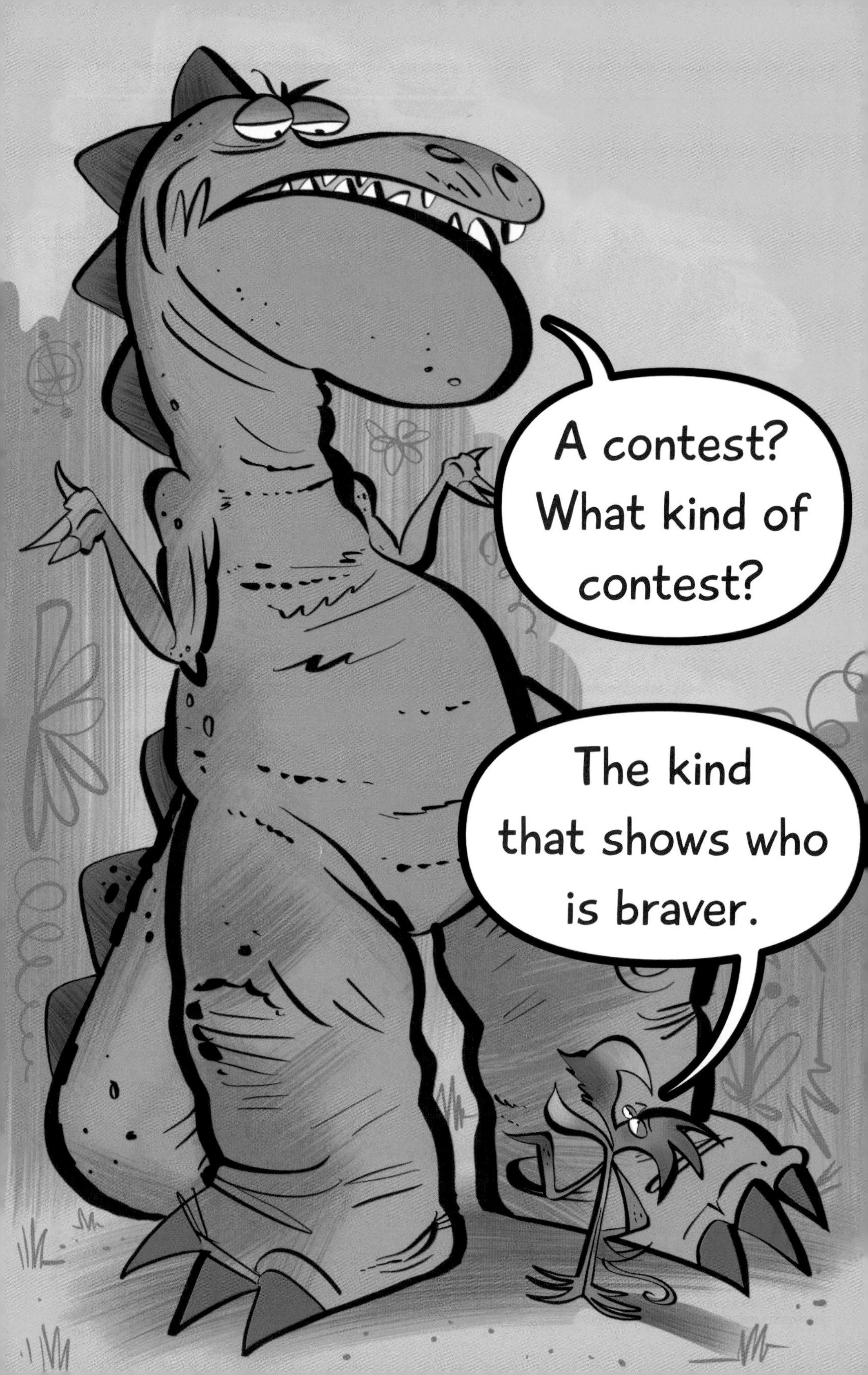
A contest? What kind of contest?
The kind that shows who is braver.

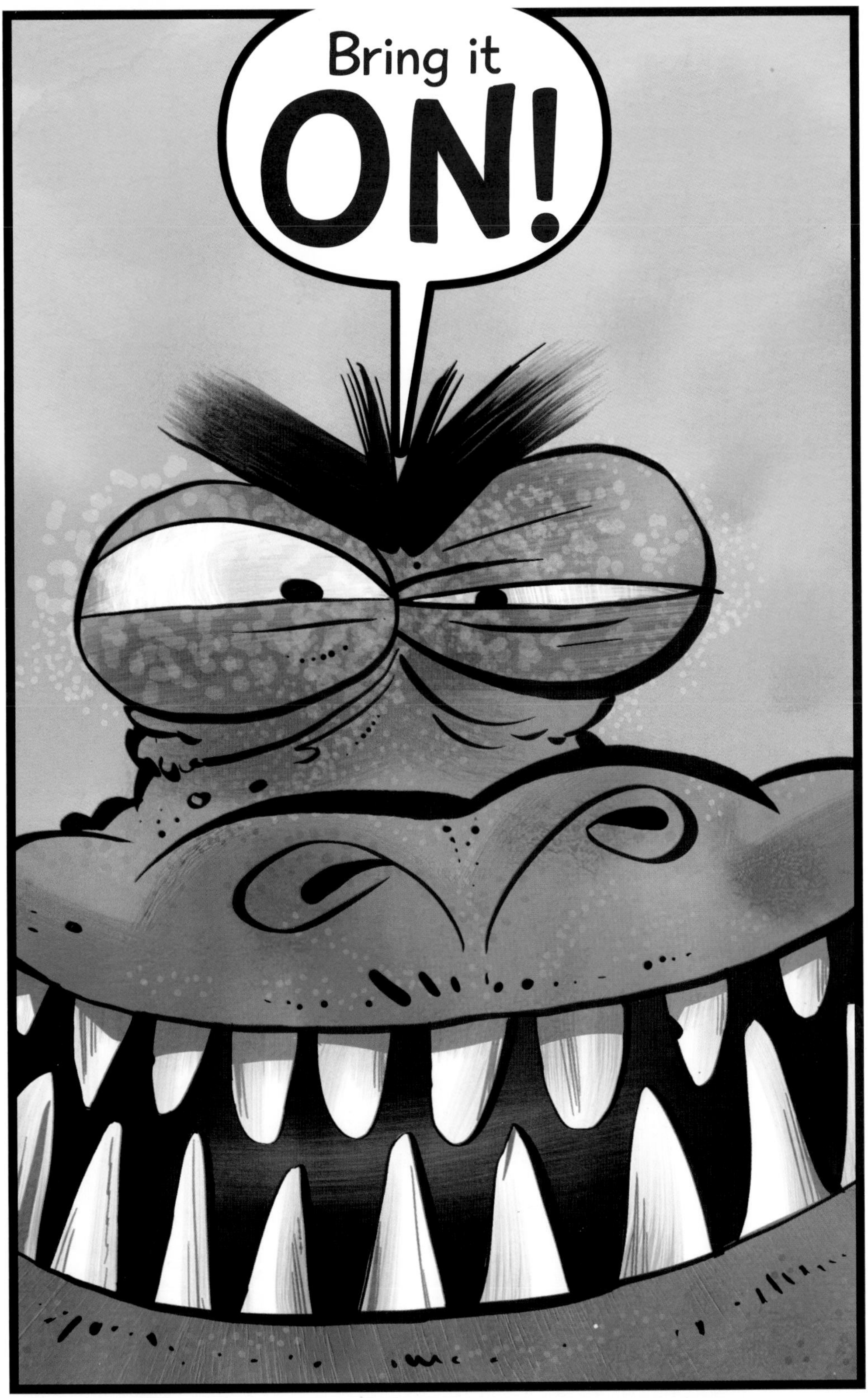
Bring it ON!

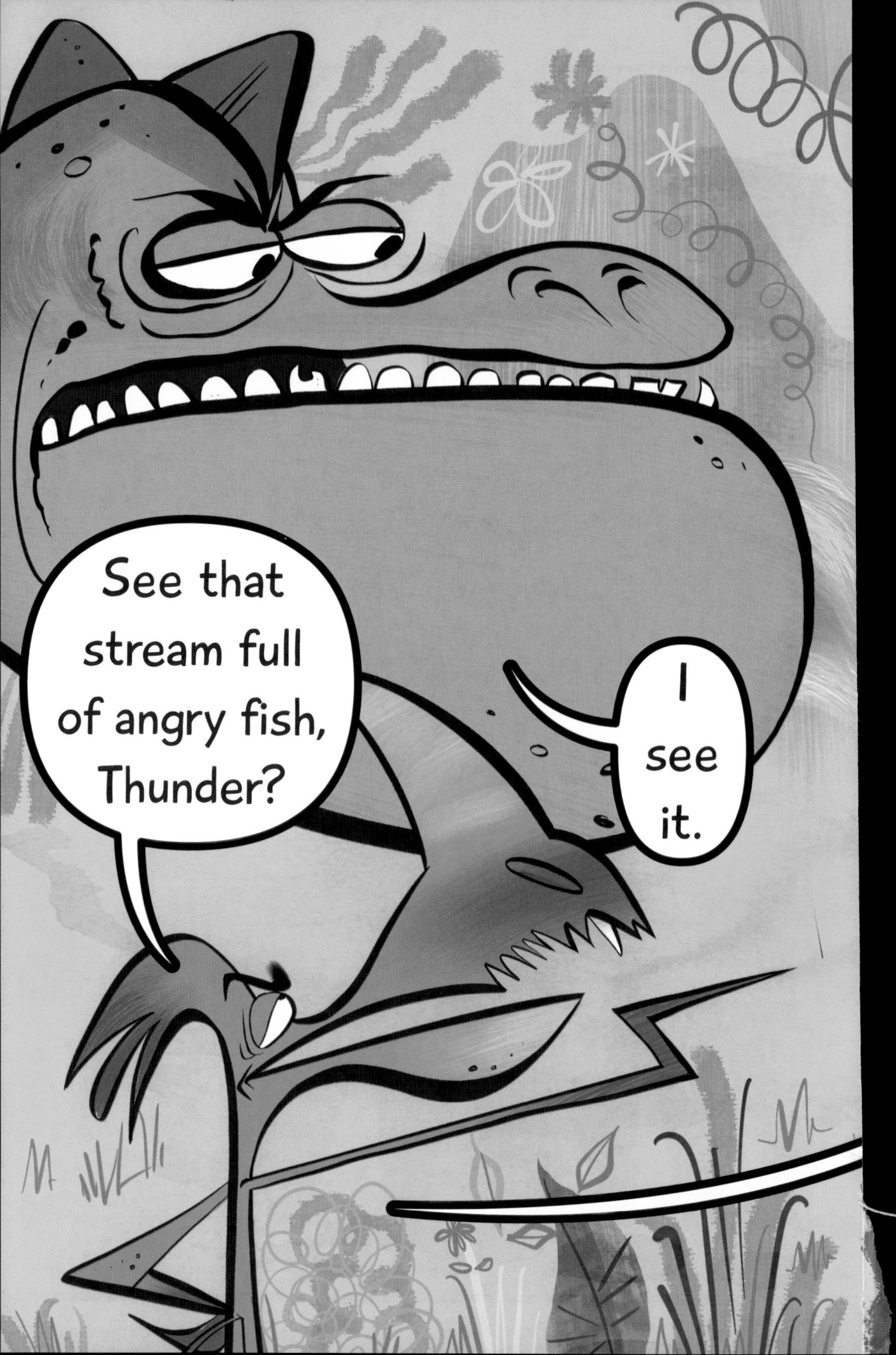
See that stream full of angry fish, Thunder?
I see it.

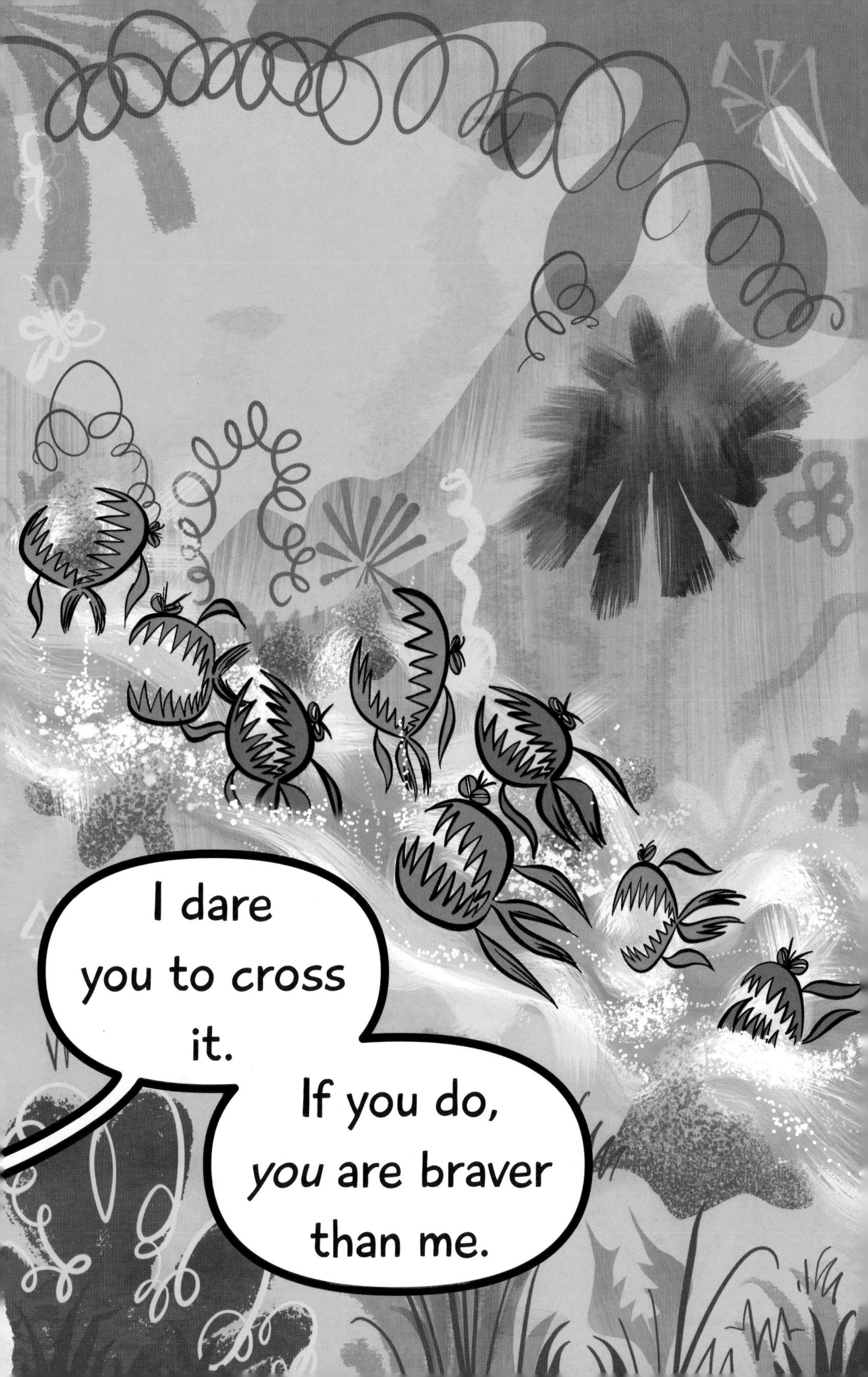
I dare you to cross it.
If you do, *you* are braver than me.

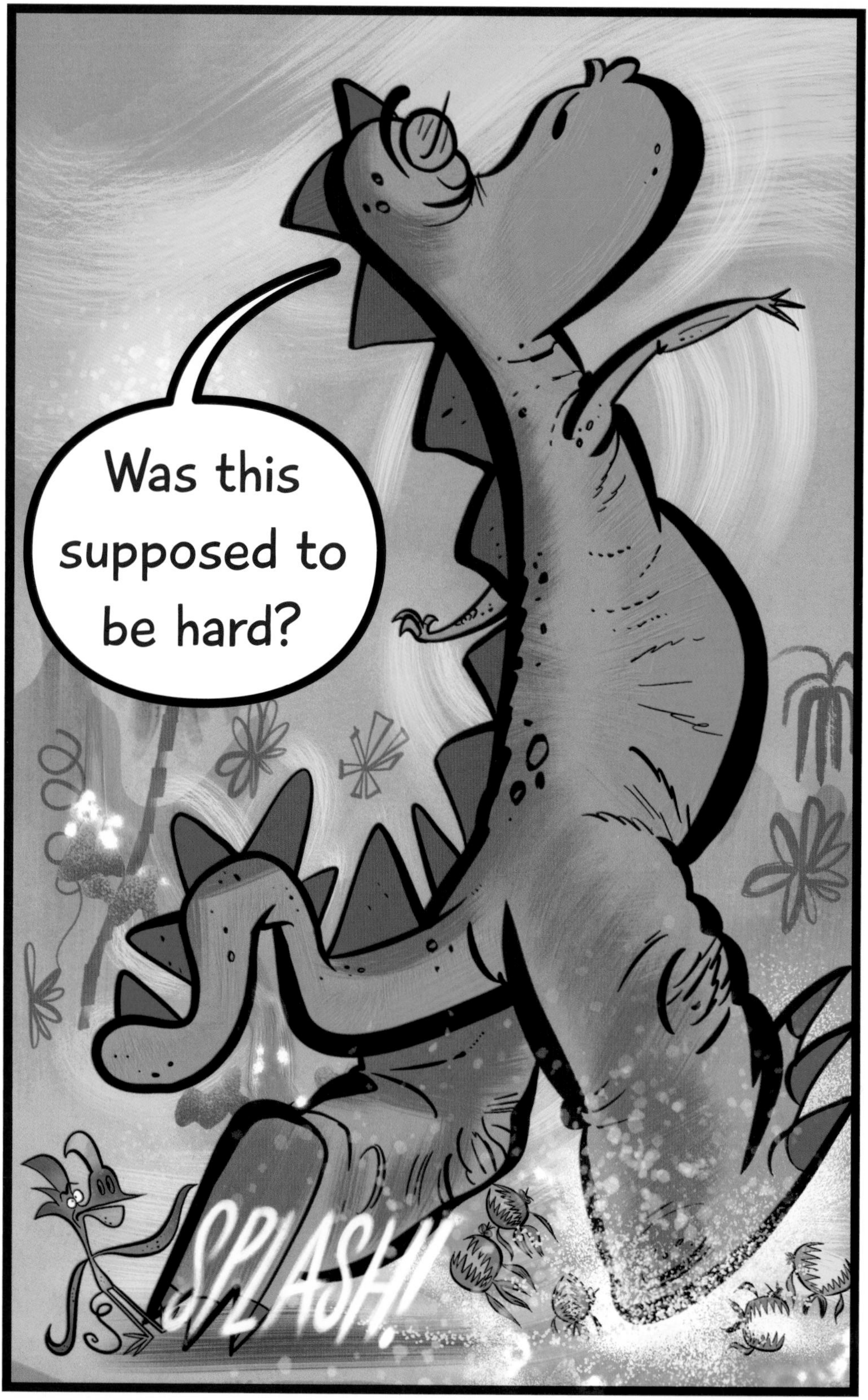
Was this supposed to be hard?
SPLASH!

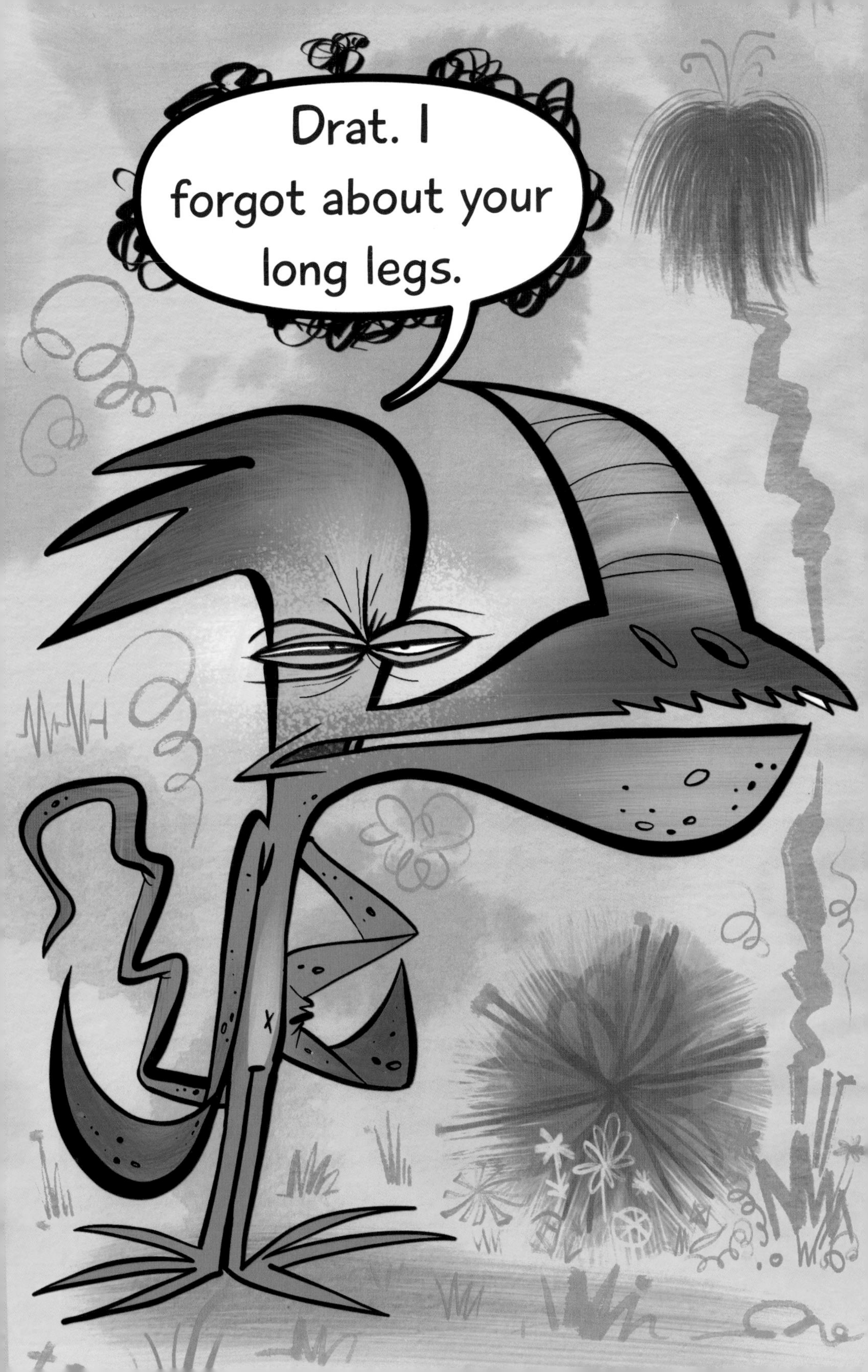
Drat. I forgot about your long legs.

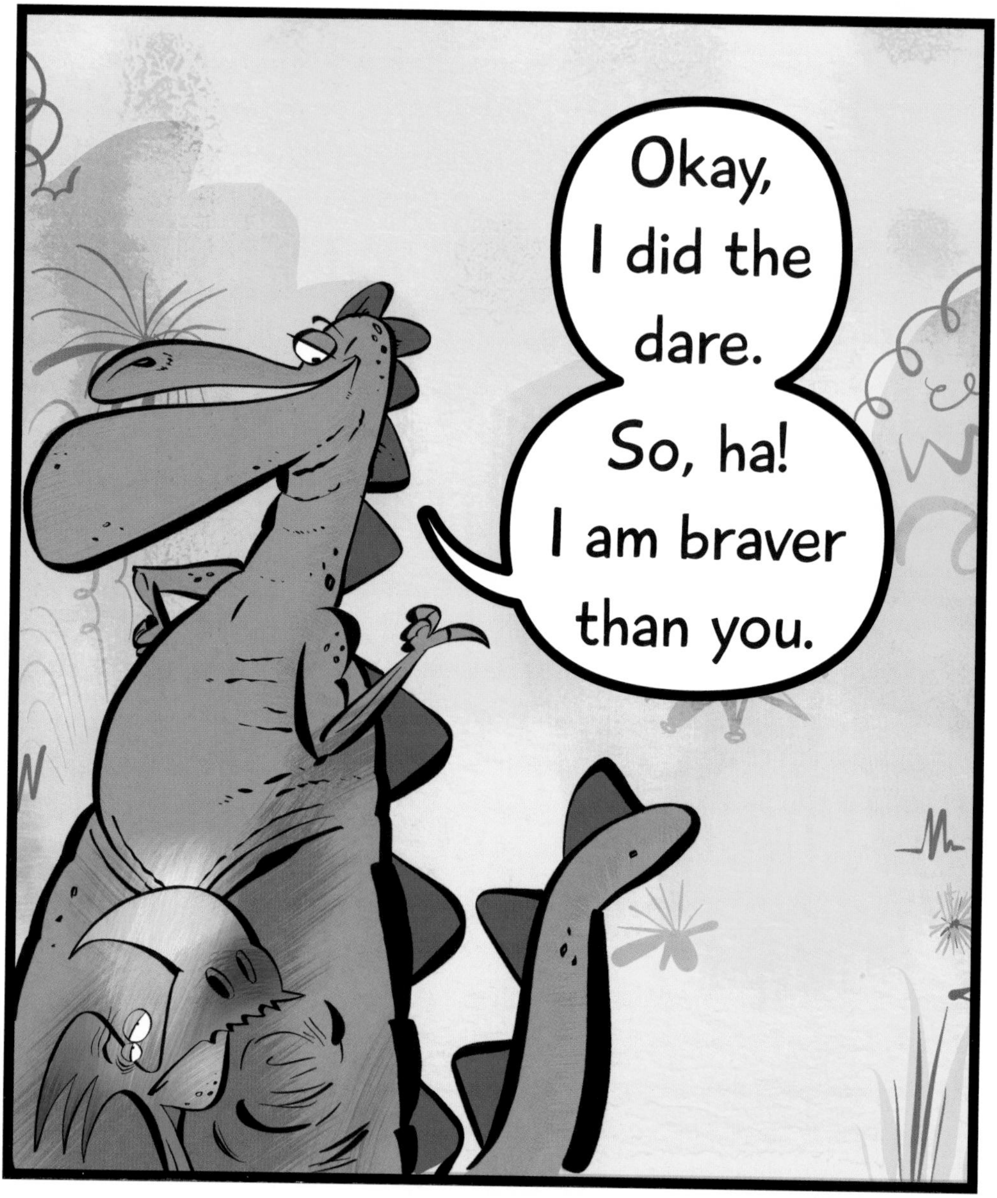
Okay, I did the dare.
So, ha! I am braver than you.

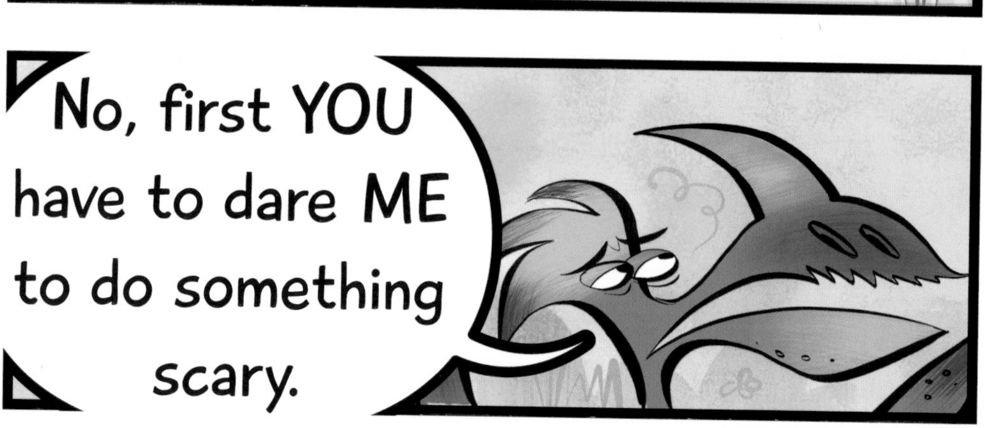
No, first YOU have to dare ME to do something scary.

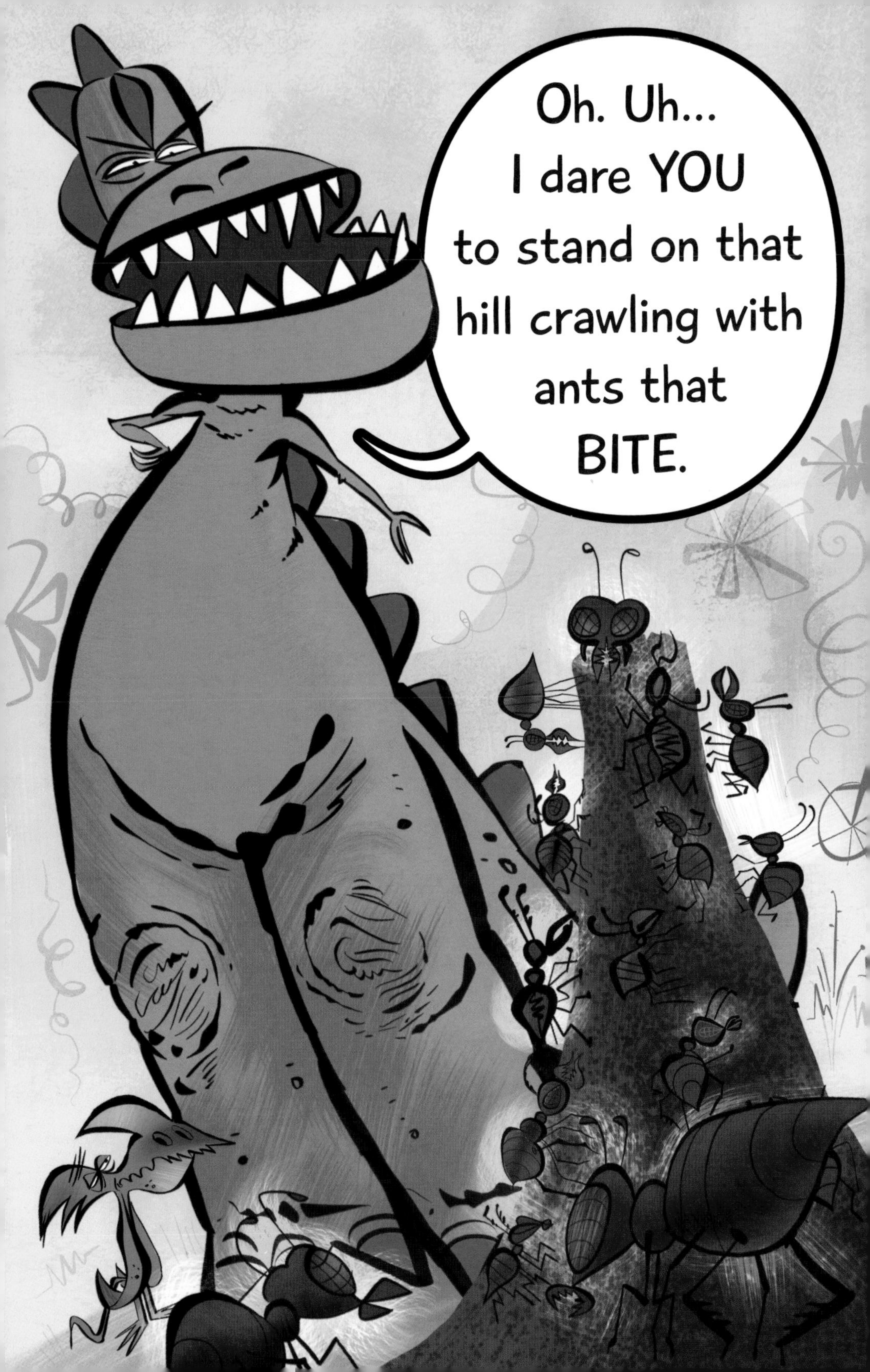
Oh. Uh... I dare YOU to stand on that hill crawling with ants that BITE.

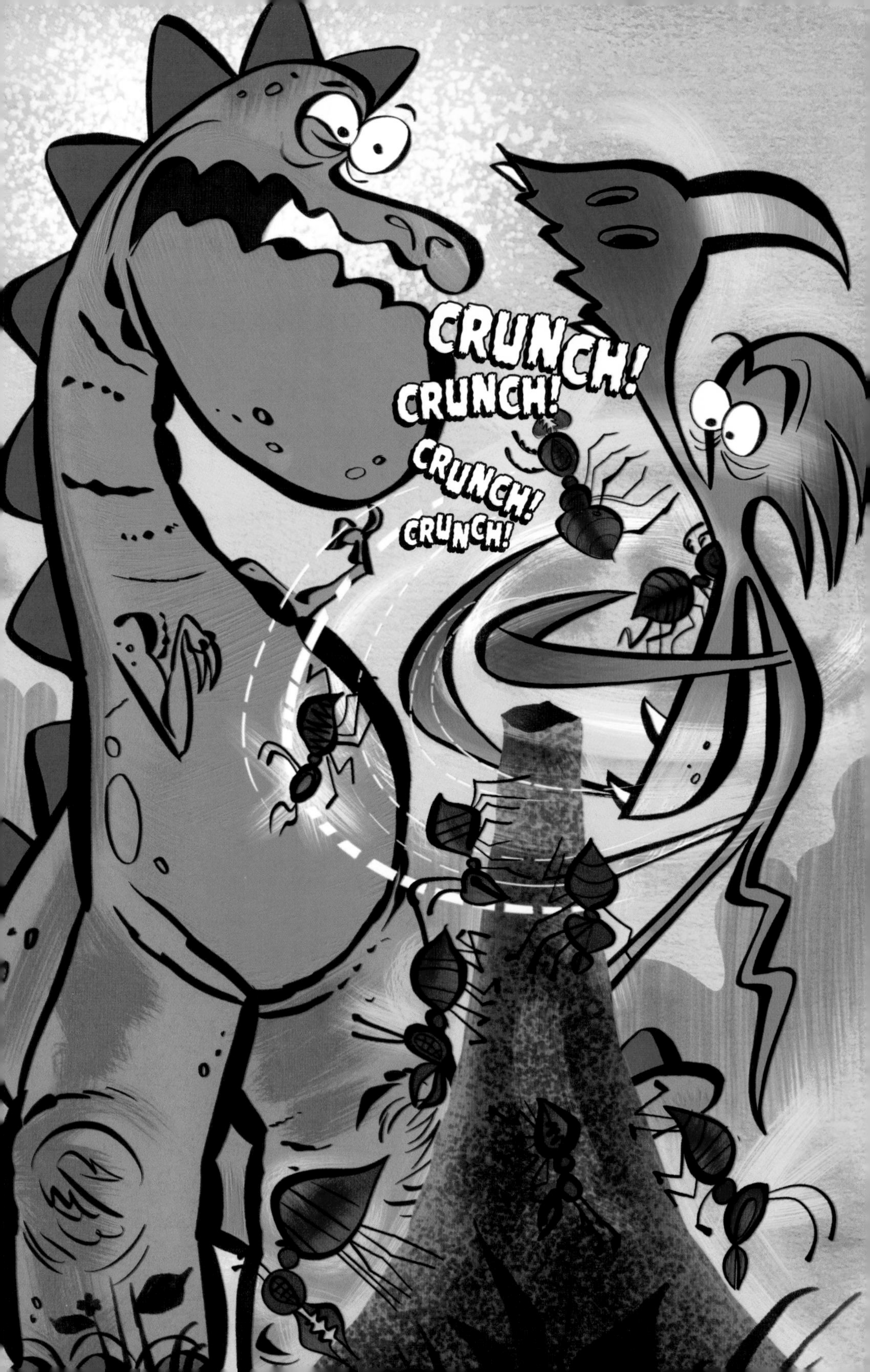
CRUNCH!
CRUNCH!
CRUNCH!
CRUNCH!

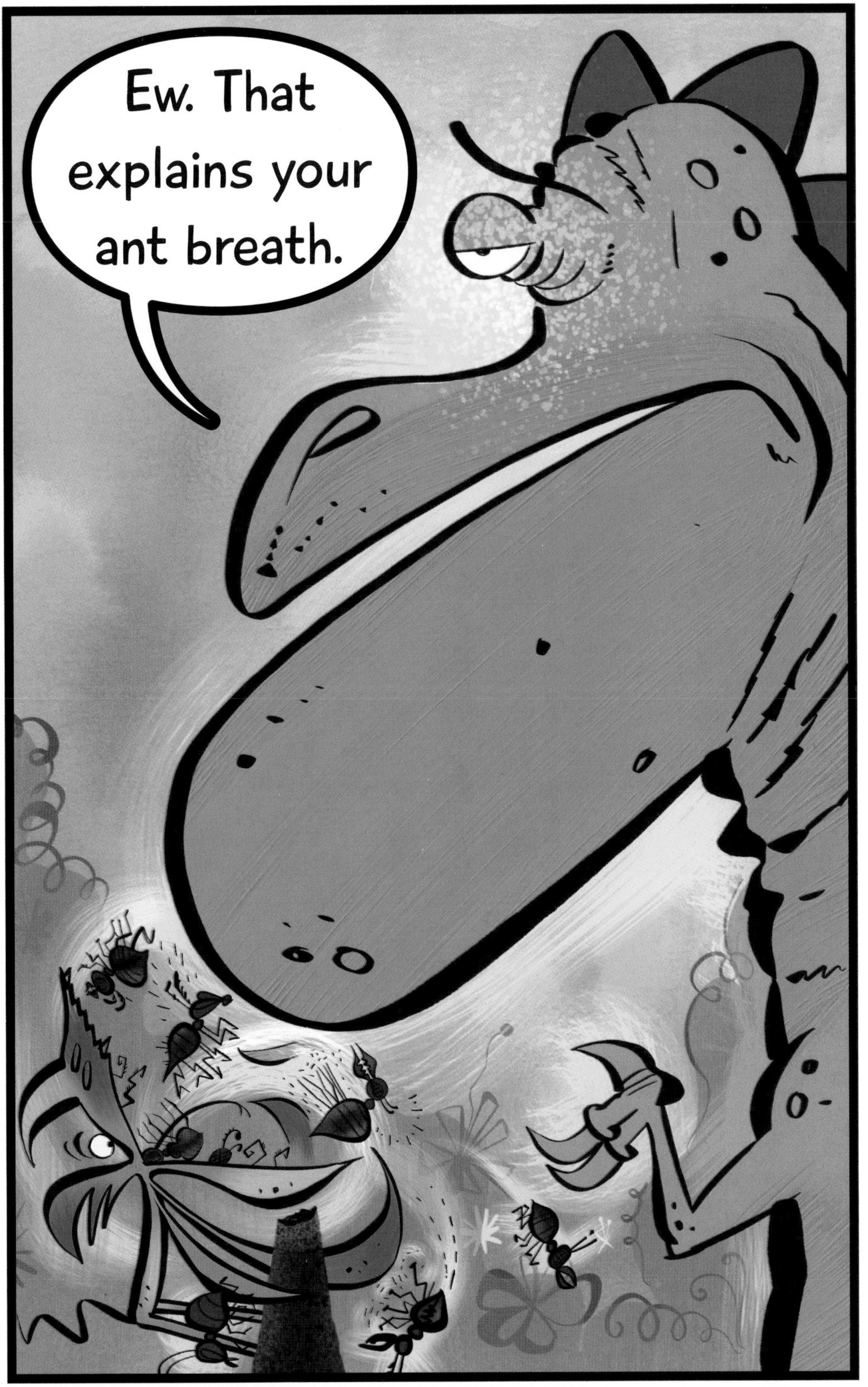
Ew. That explains your ant breath.

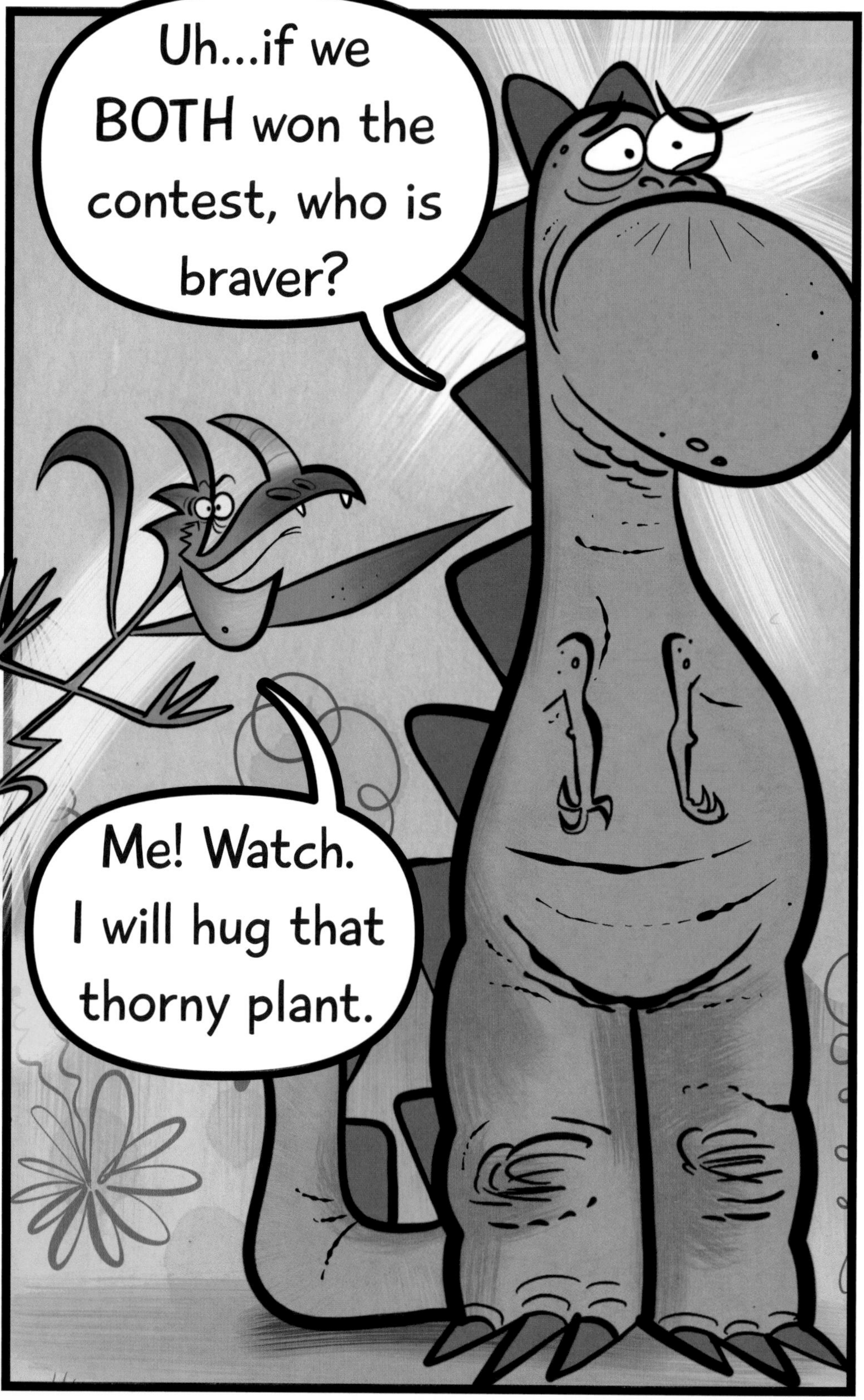
Uh...if we BOTH won the contest, who is braver?
Me! Watch. I will hug that thorny plant.

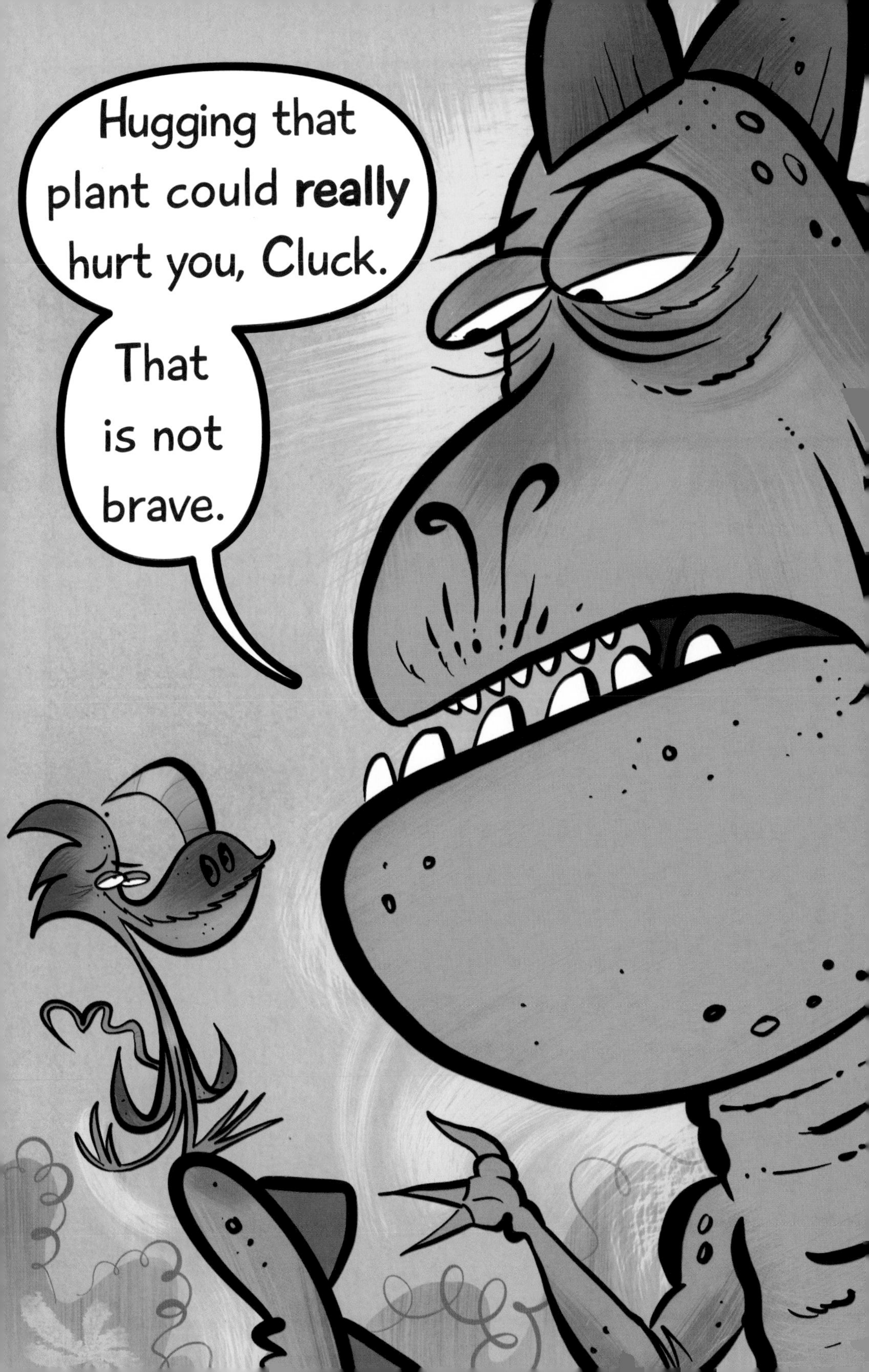
Hugging that plant could **really** hurt you, Cluck.
That is not brave.

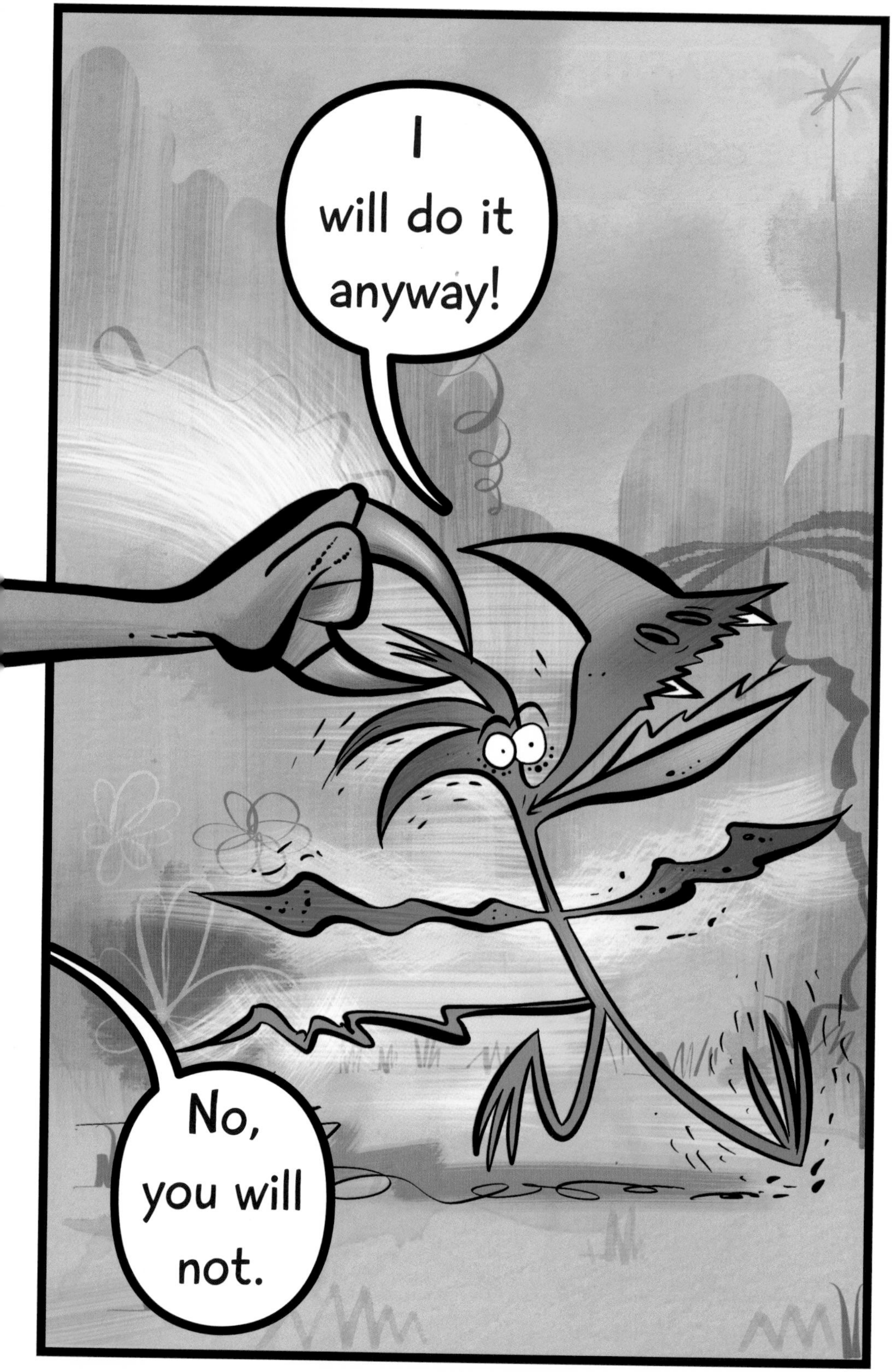
I will do it anyway!
No, you will not.

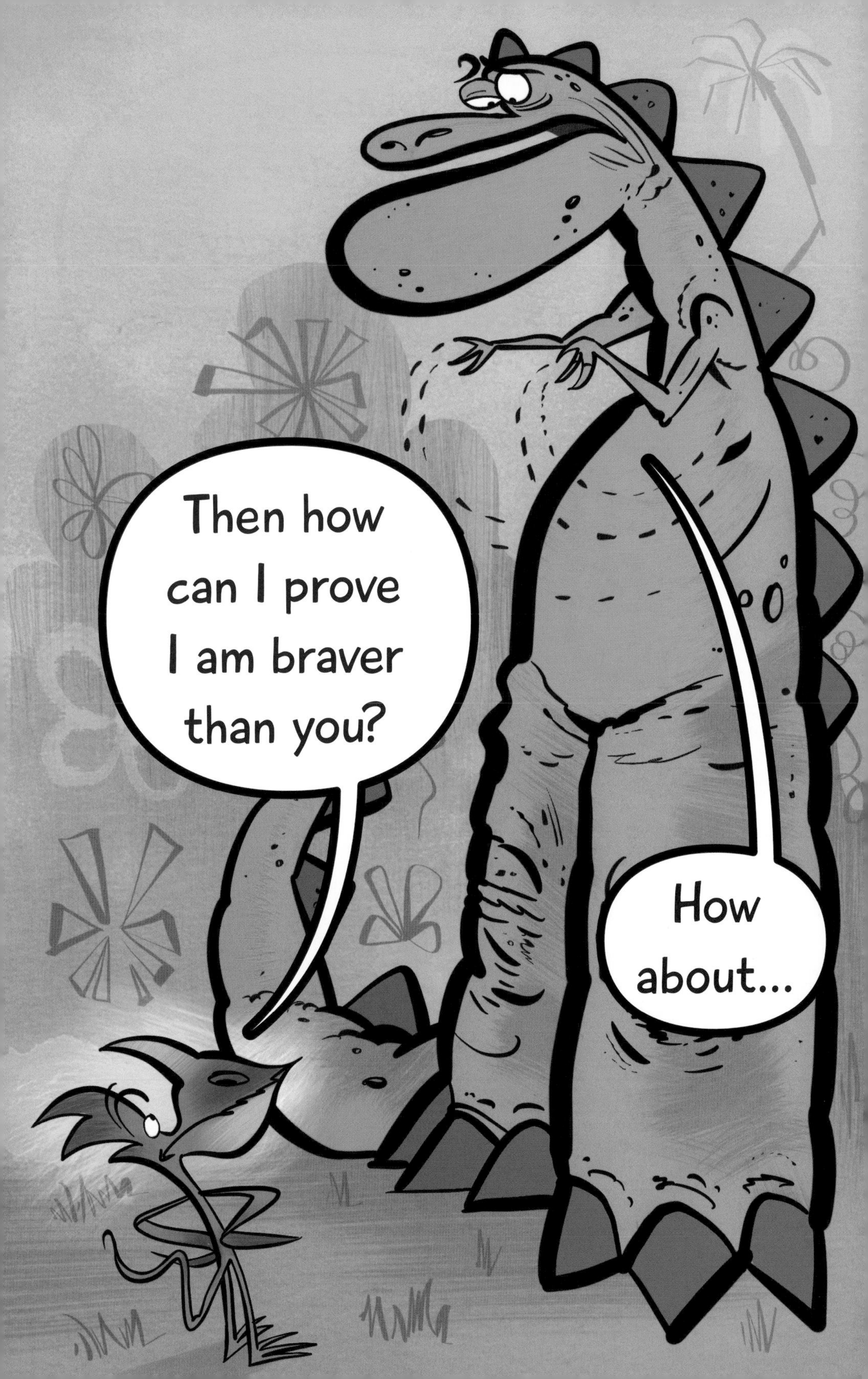
Then how can I prove I am braver than you?
How about...

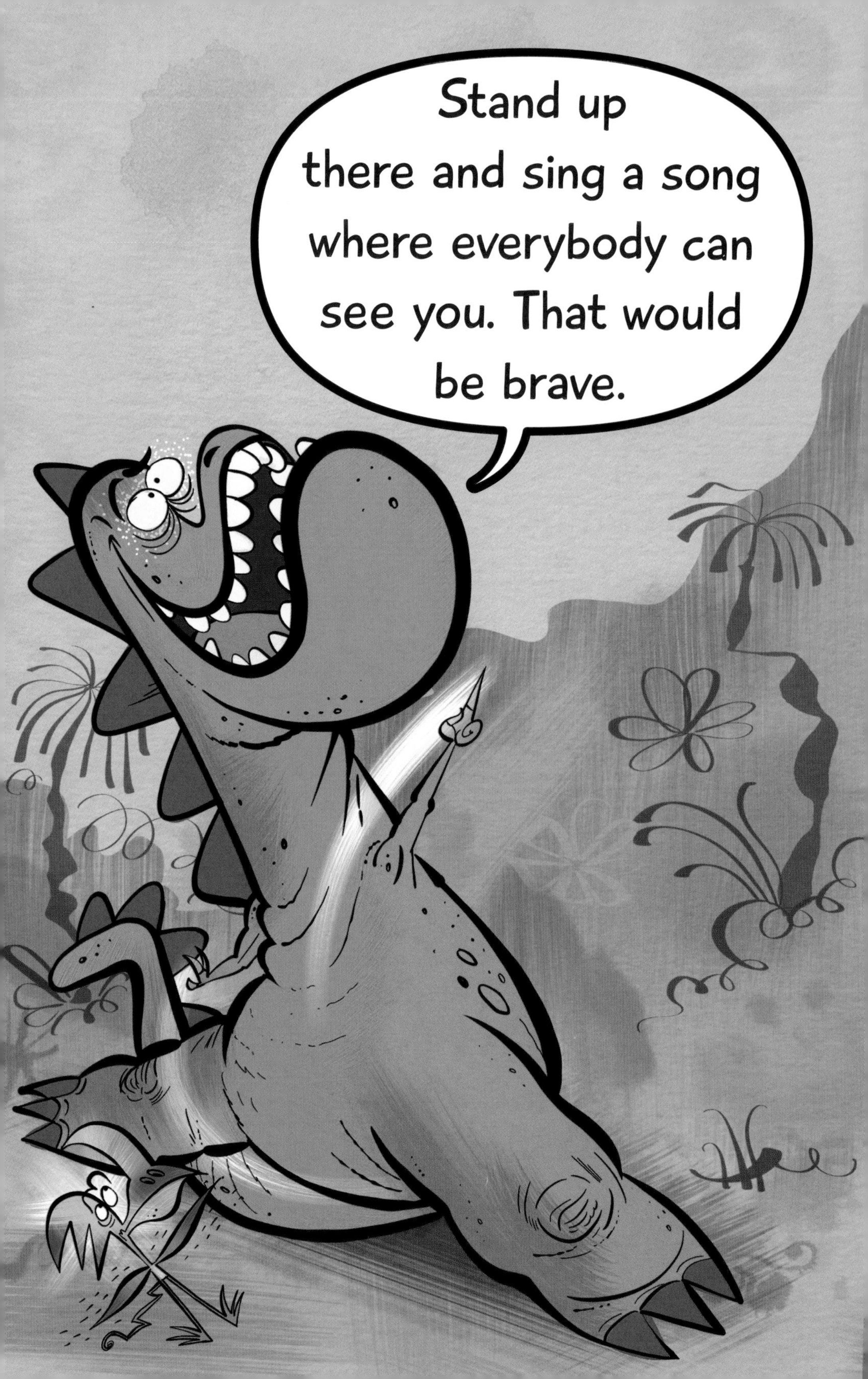
Stand up there and sing a song where everybody can see you. That would be brave.

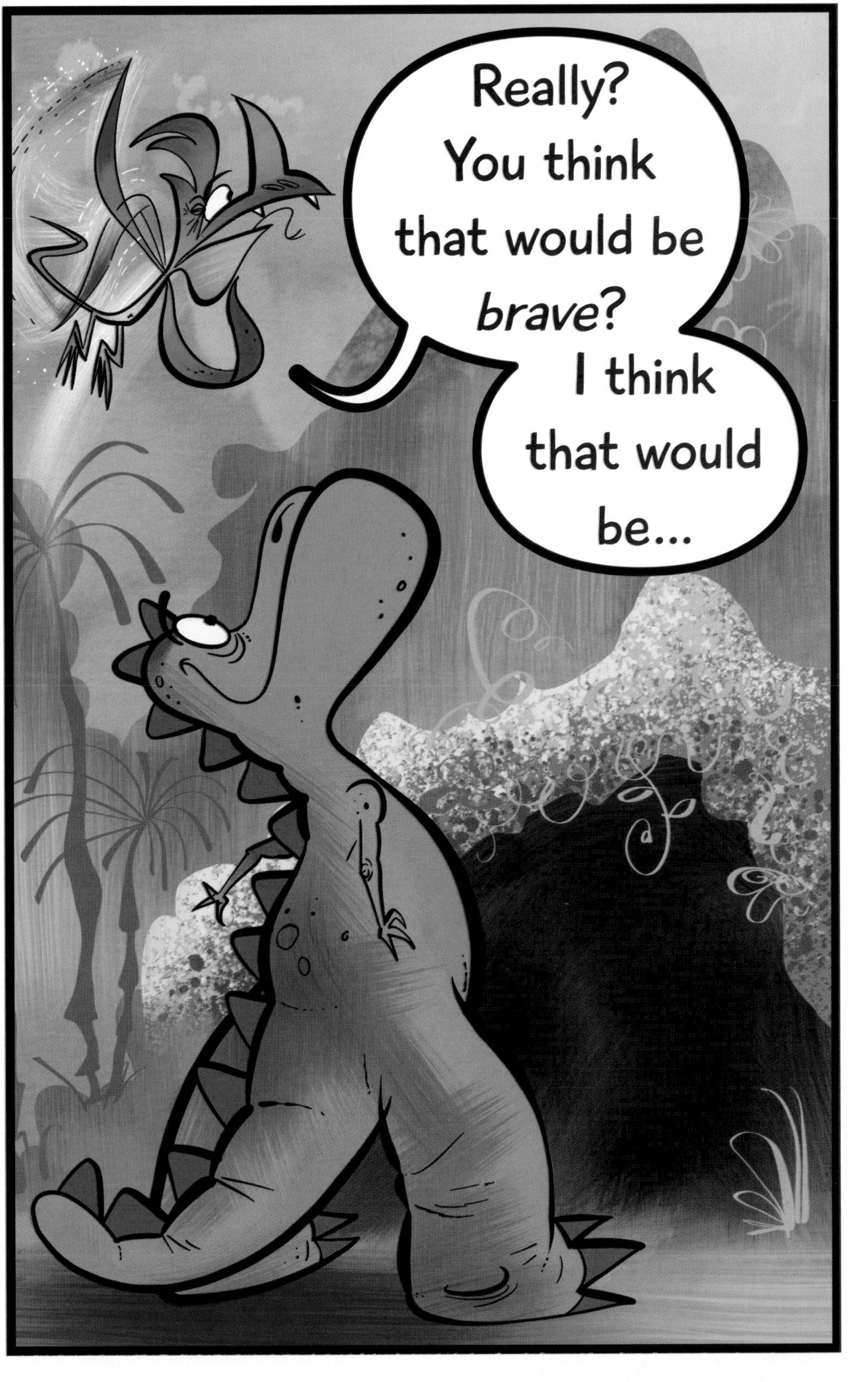
Really? You think that would be *brave*?
I think that would be...

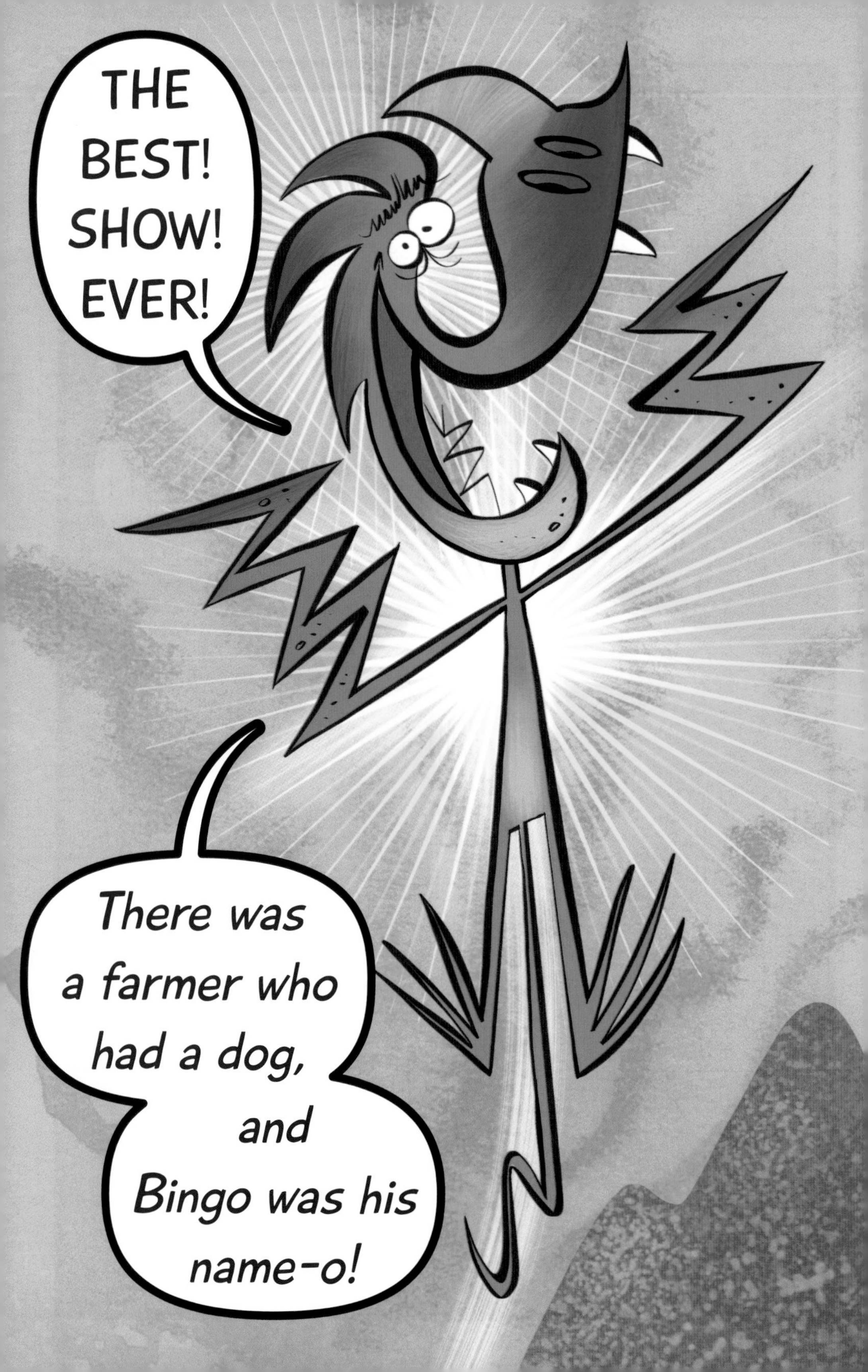
THE BEST! SHOW! EVER!
There was a farmer who had a dog, and Bingo was his name-o!

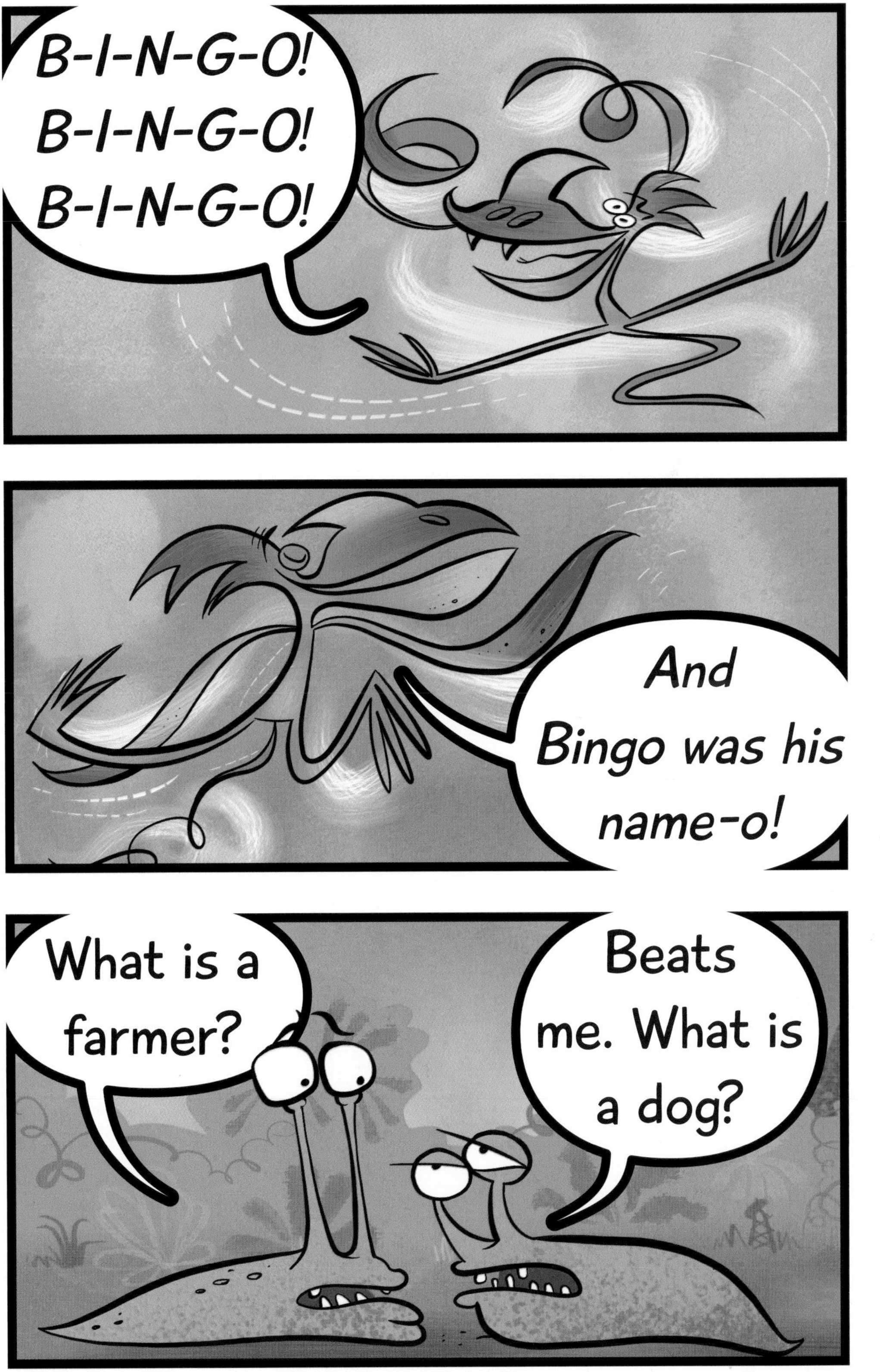
B-I-N-G-O!
B-I-N-G-O!
B-I-N-G-O!
And Bingo was his name-o!
What is a farmer?
Beats me. What is a dog?

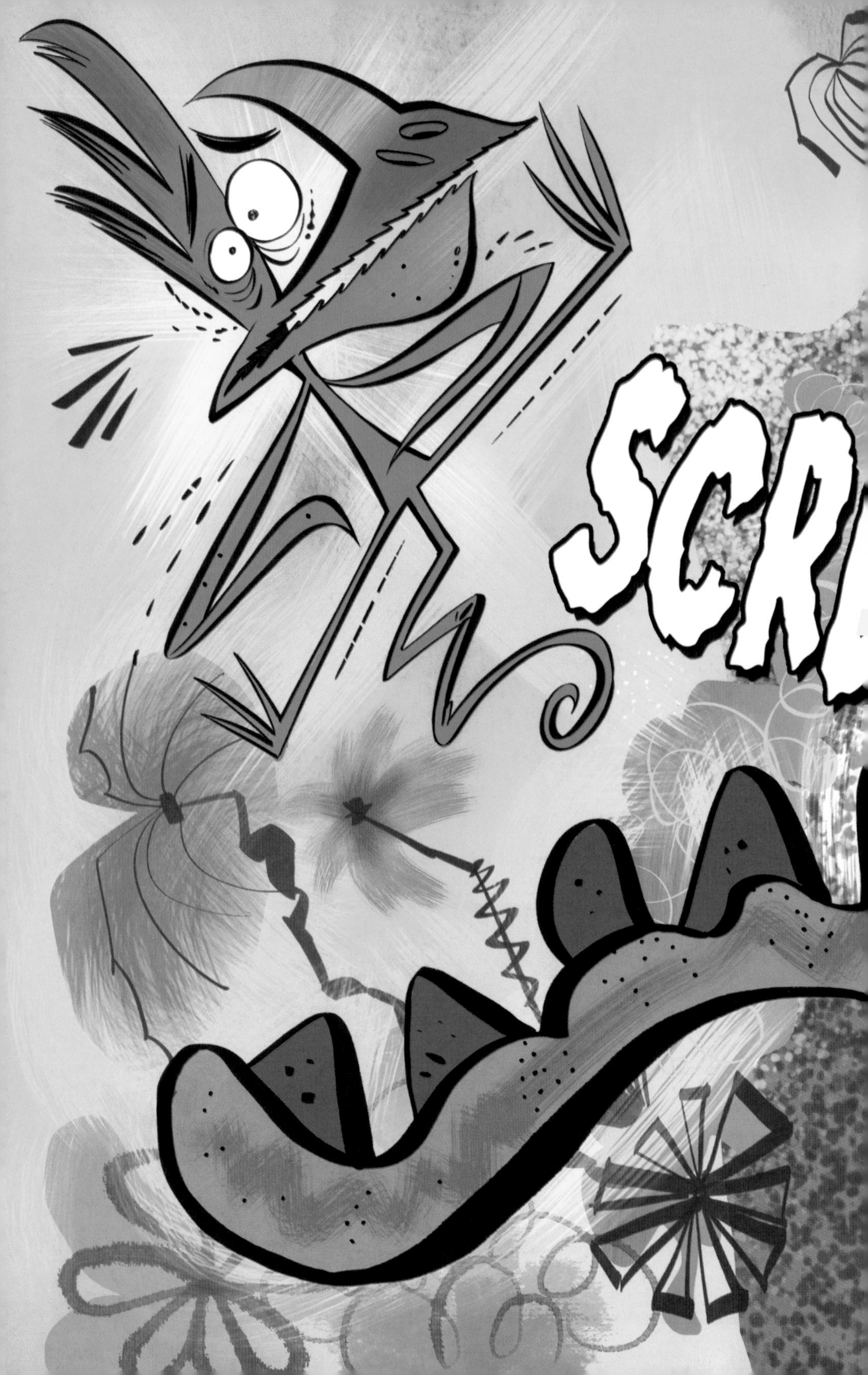
SCR

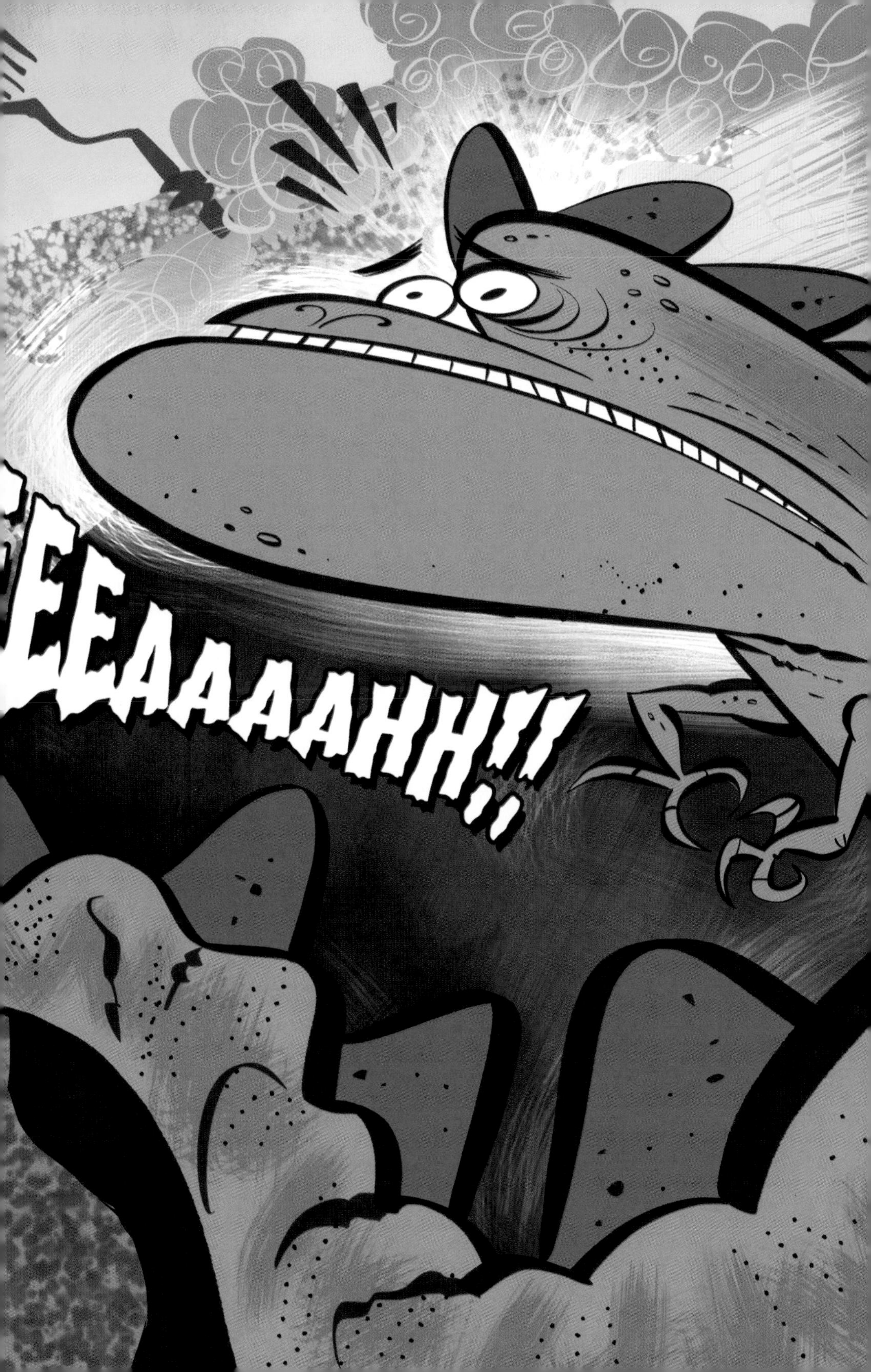
EEAAAAAHH!!

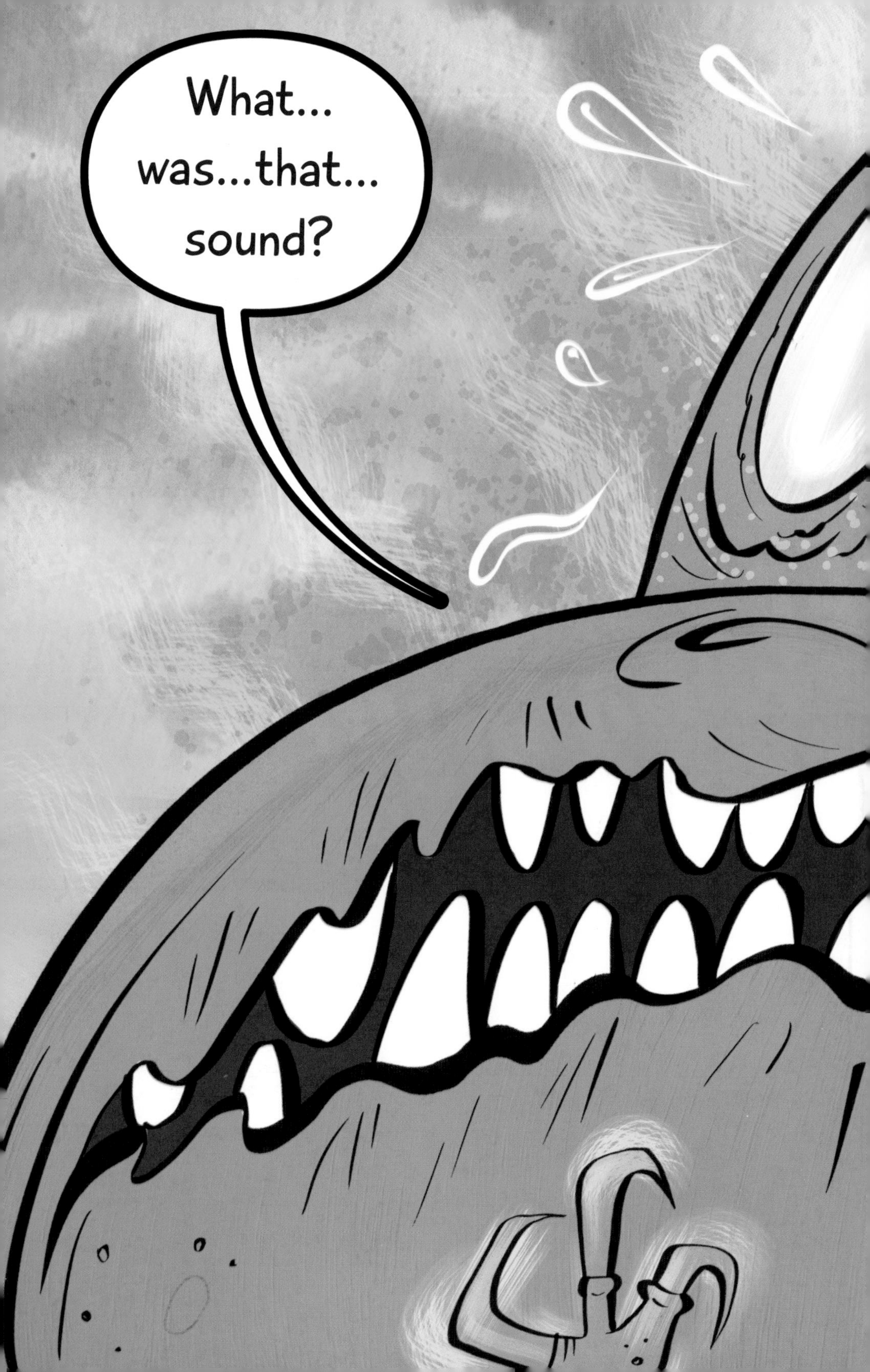
What... was...that... sound?

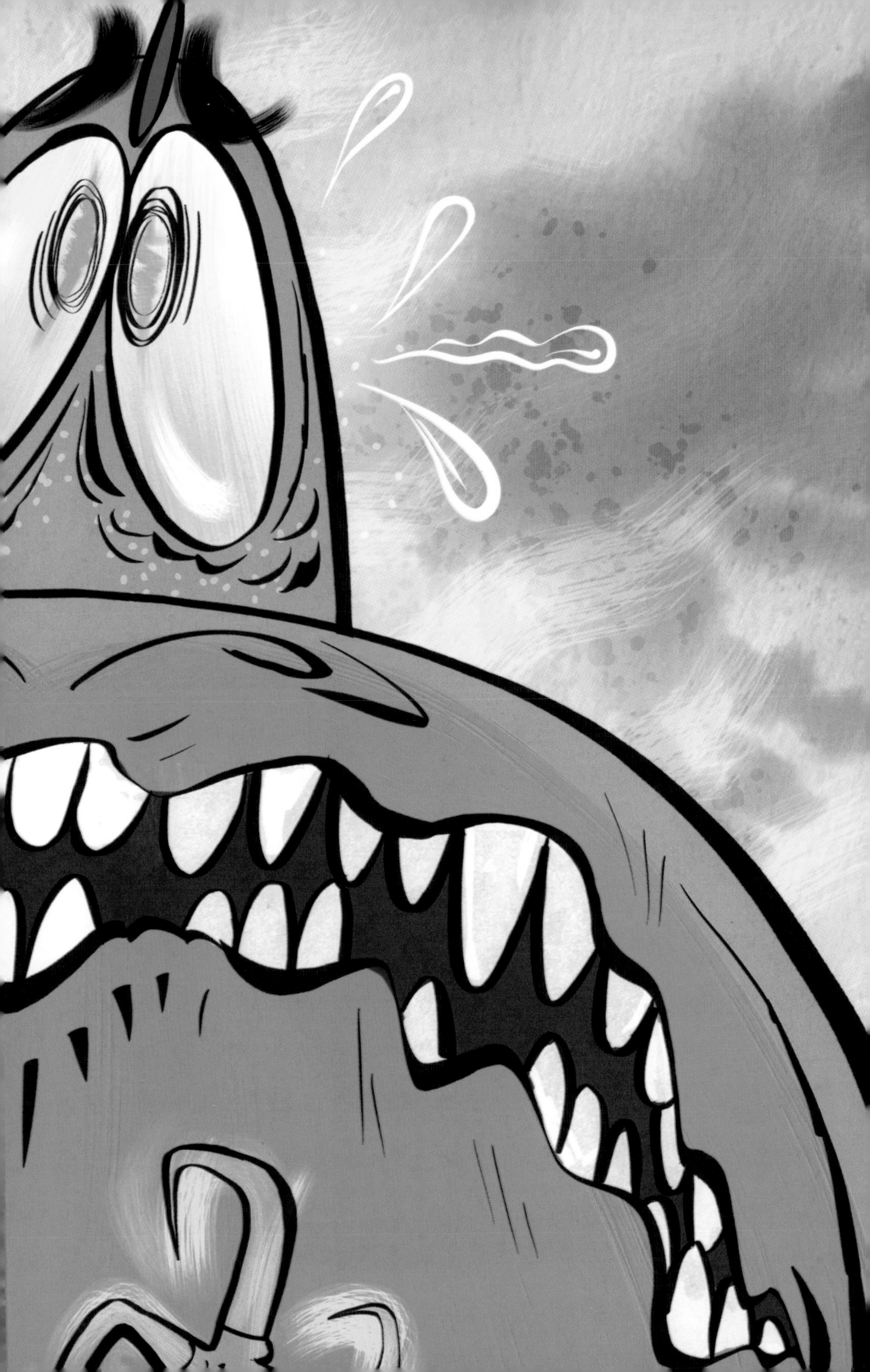

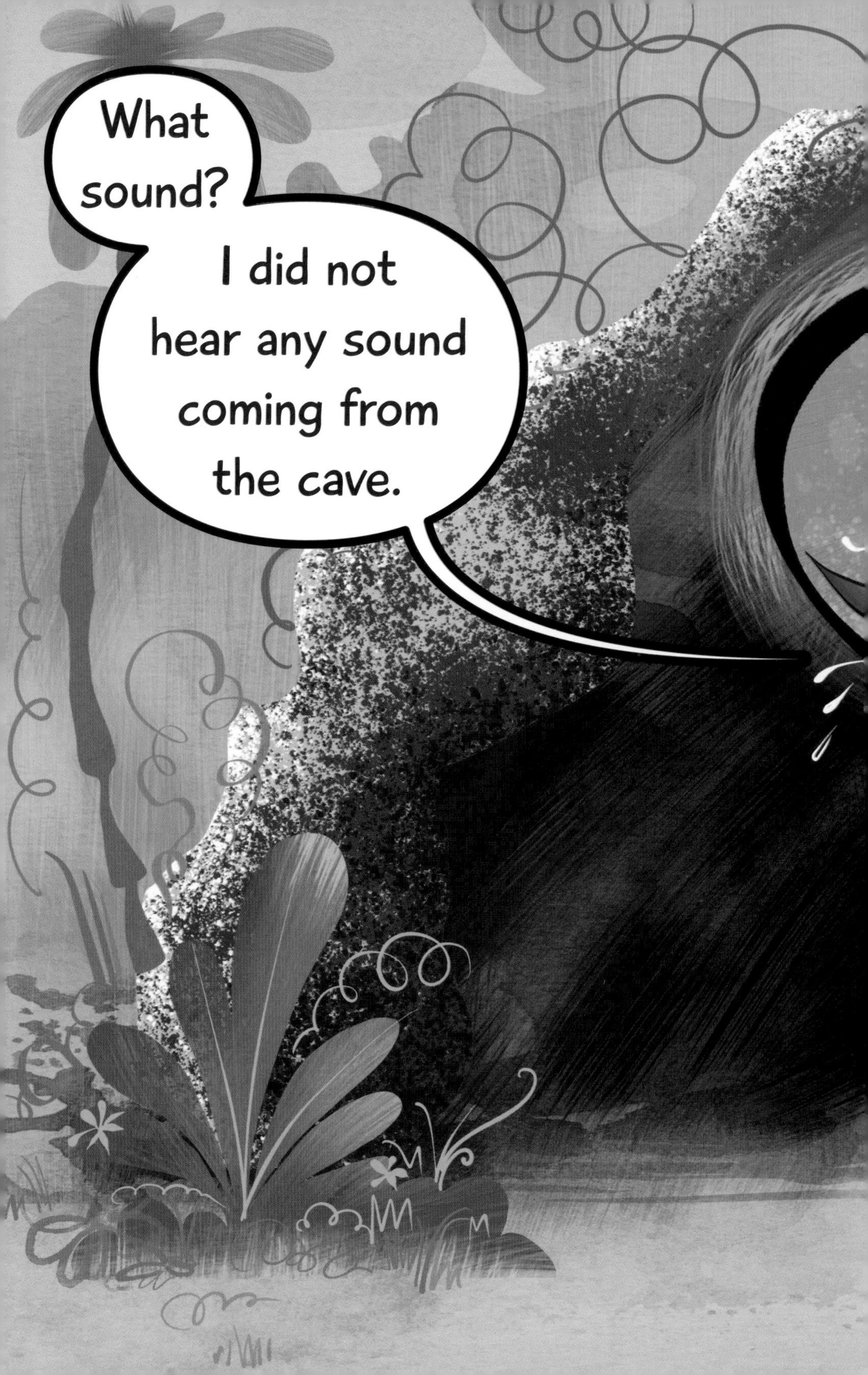
What sound?
I did not hear any sound coming from the cave.

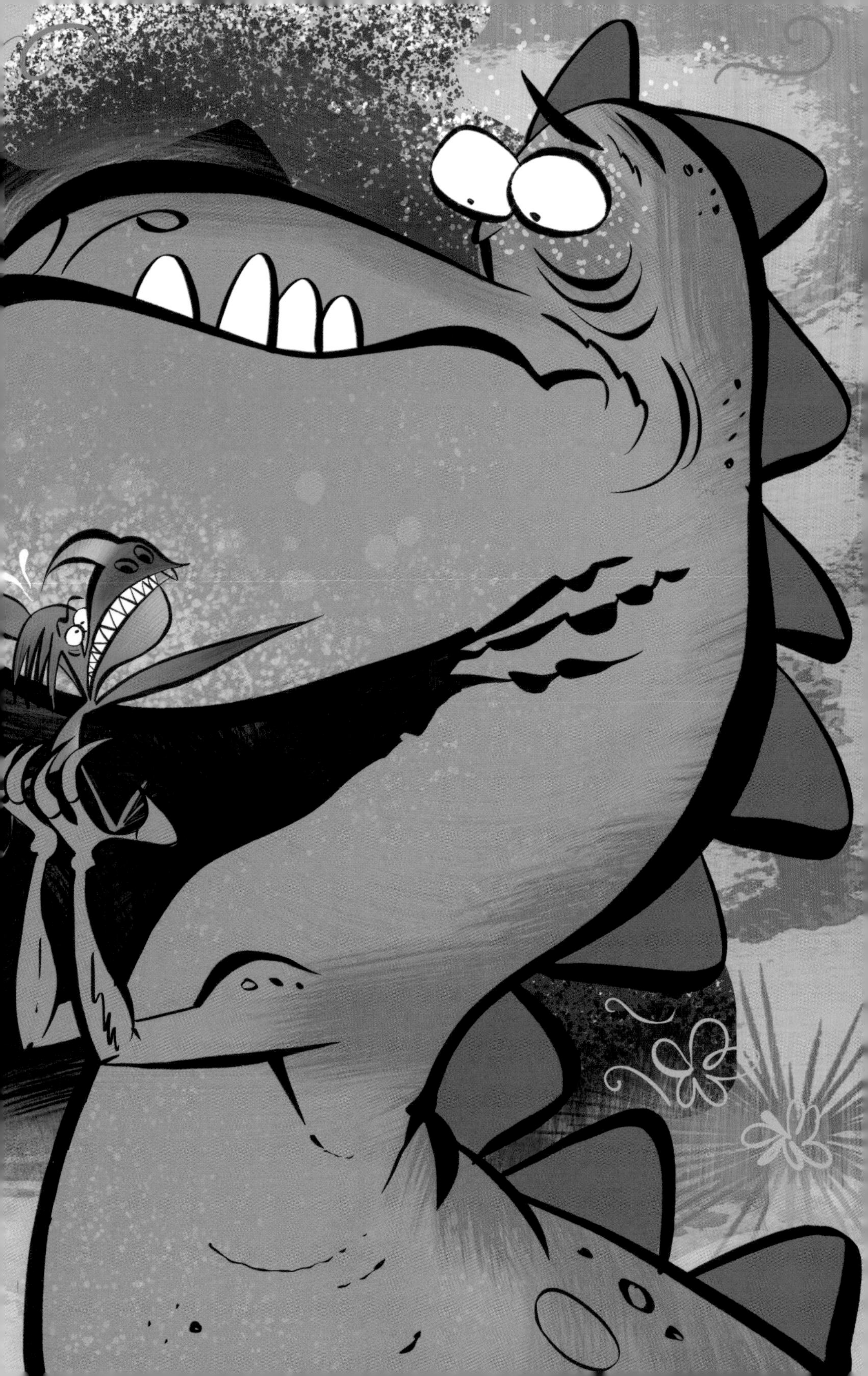

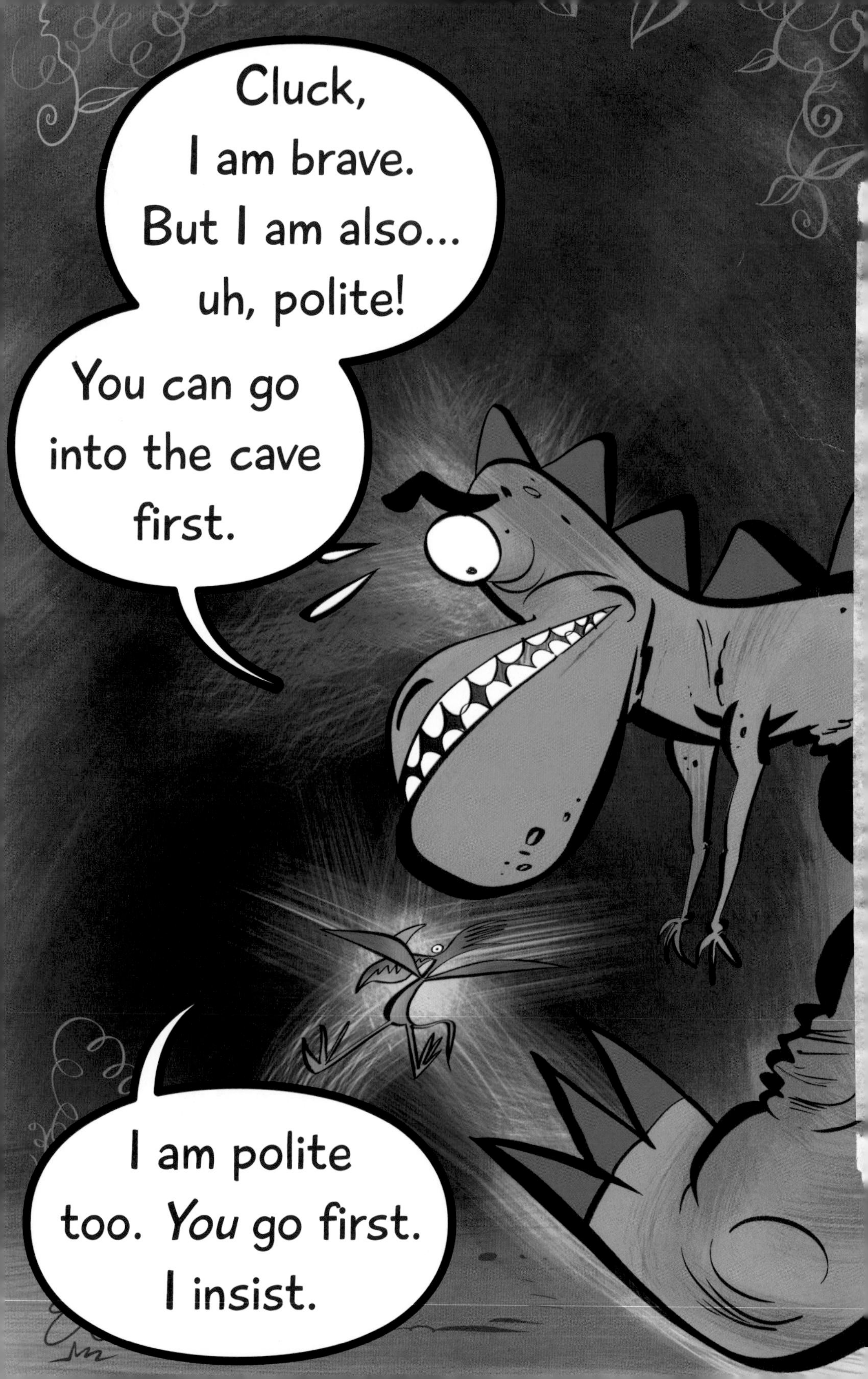
Cluck, I am brave. But I am also... uh, polite!
You can go into the cave first.
I am polite too. *You* go first. I insist.

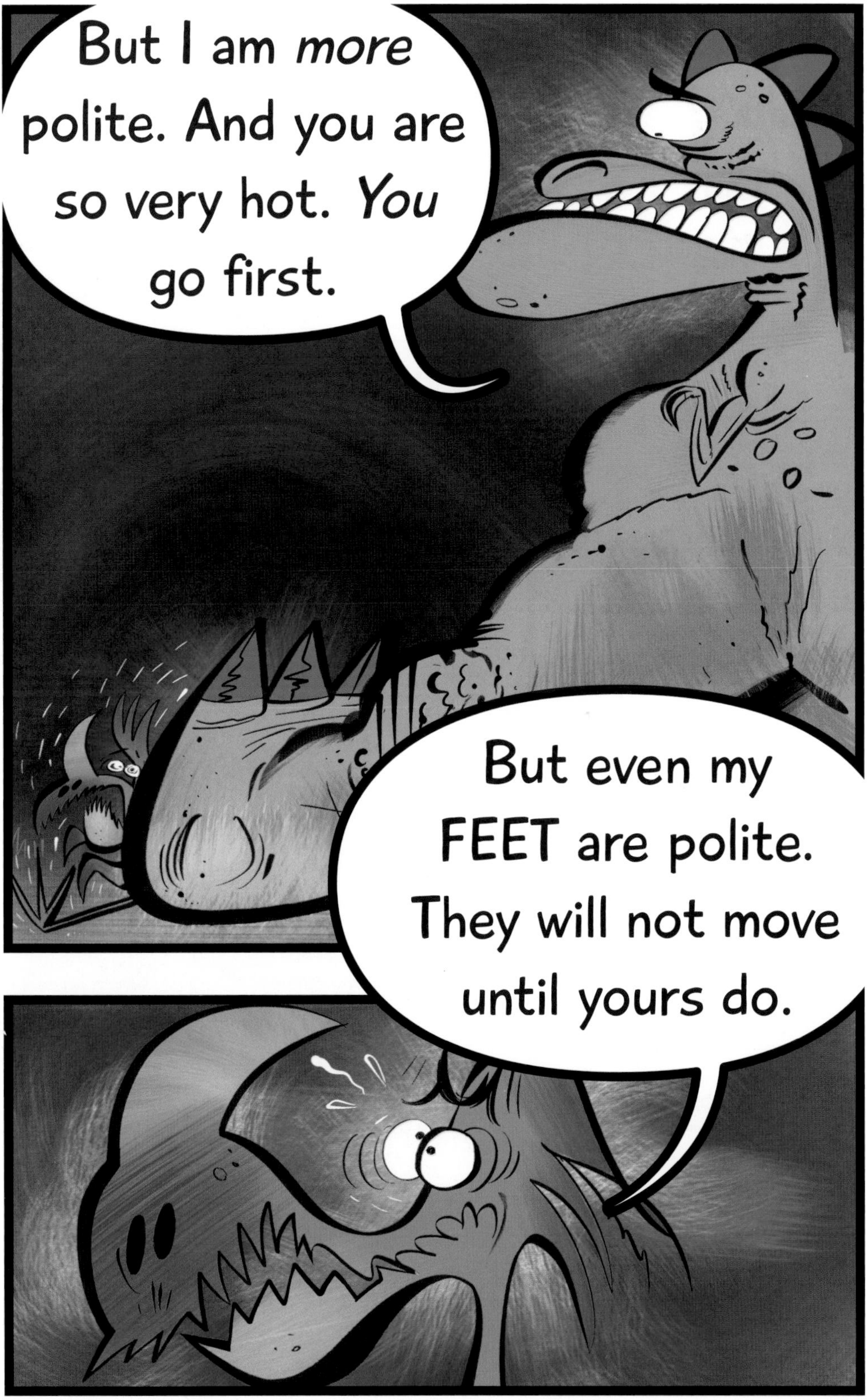
But I am *more* polite. And you are so very hot. *You* go first.
But even my FEET are polite. They will not move until yours do.

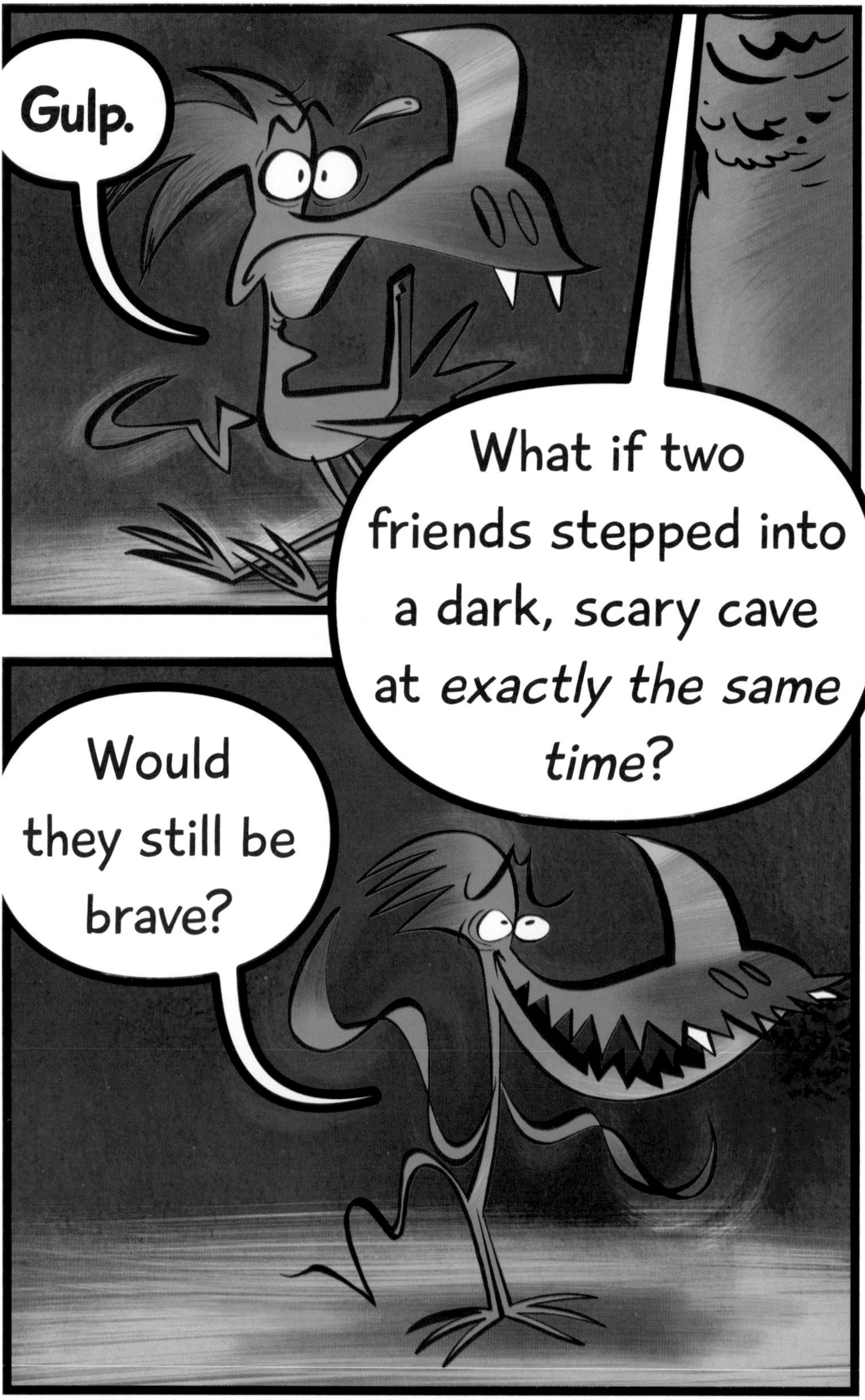
Gulp.
What if two friends stepped into a dark, scary cave at *exactly the same time*?
Would they still be brave?

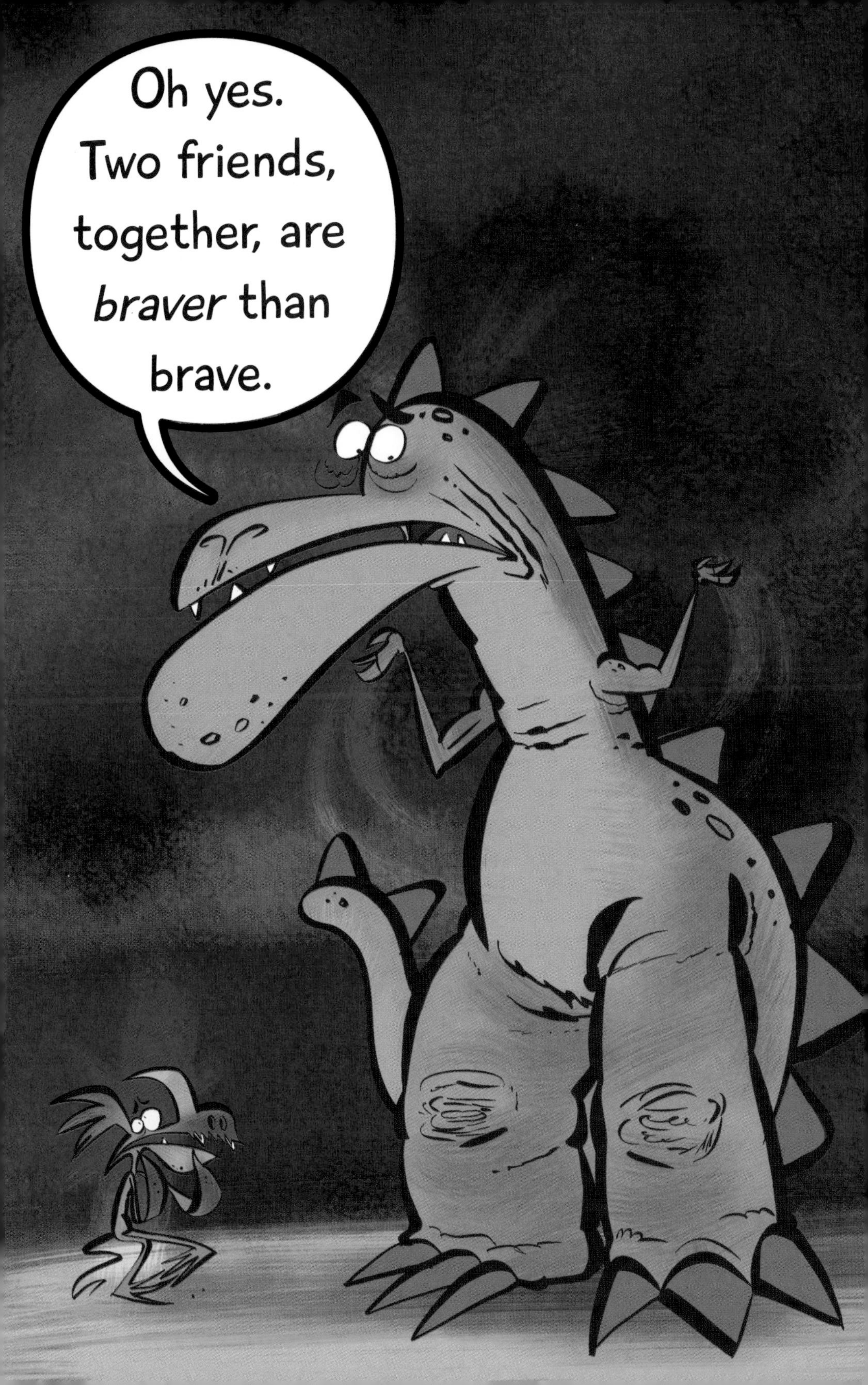
Oh yes. Two friends, together, are *braver* than brave.

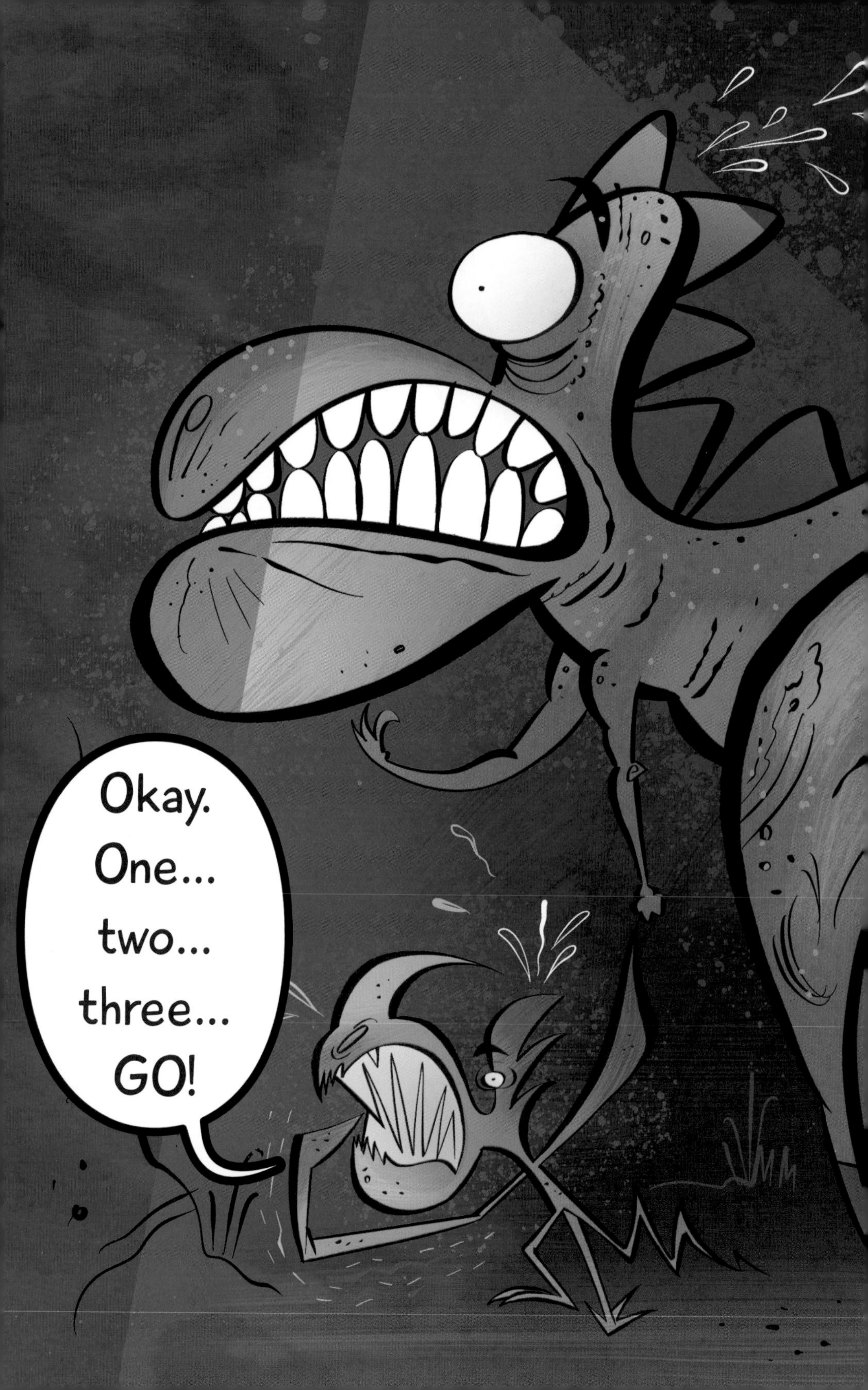
Okay. One... two... three... GO!

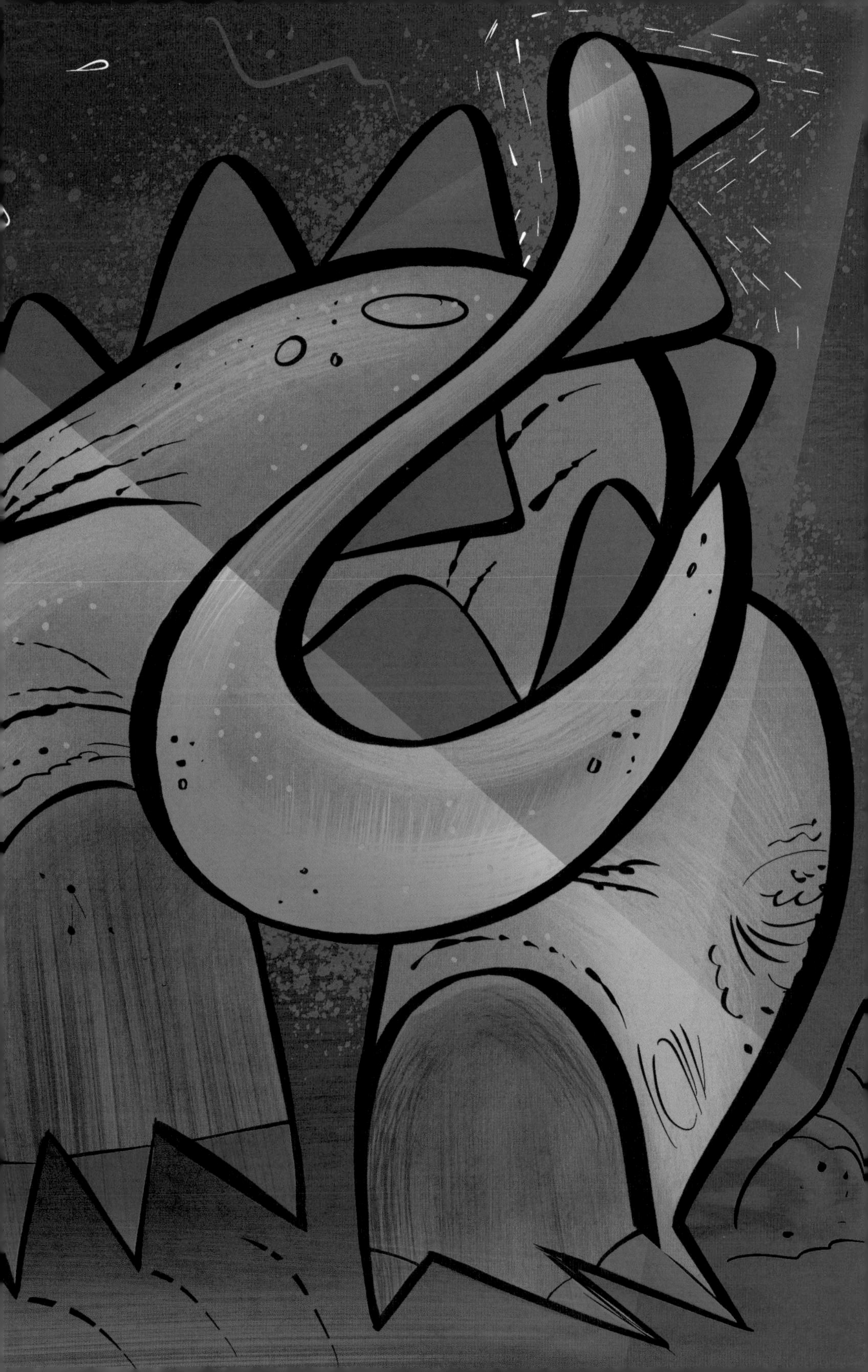

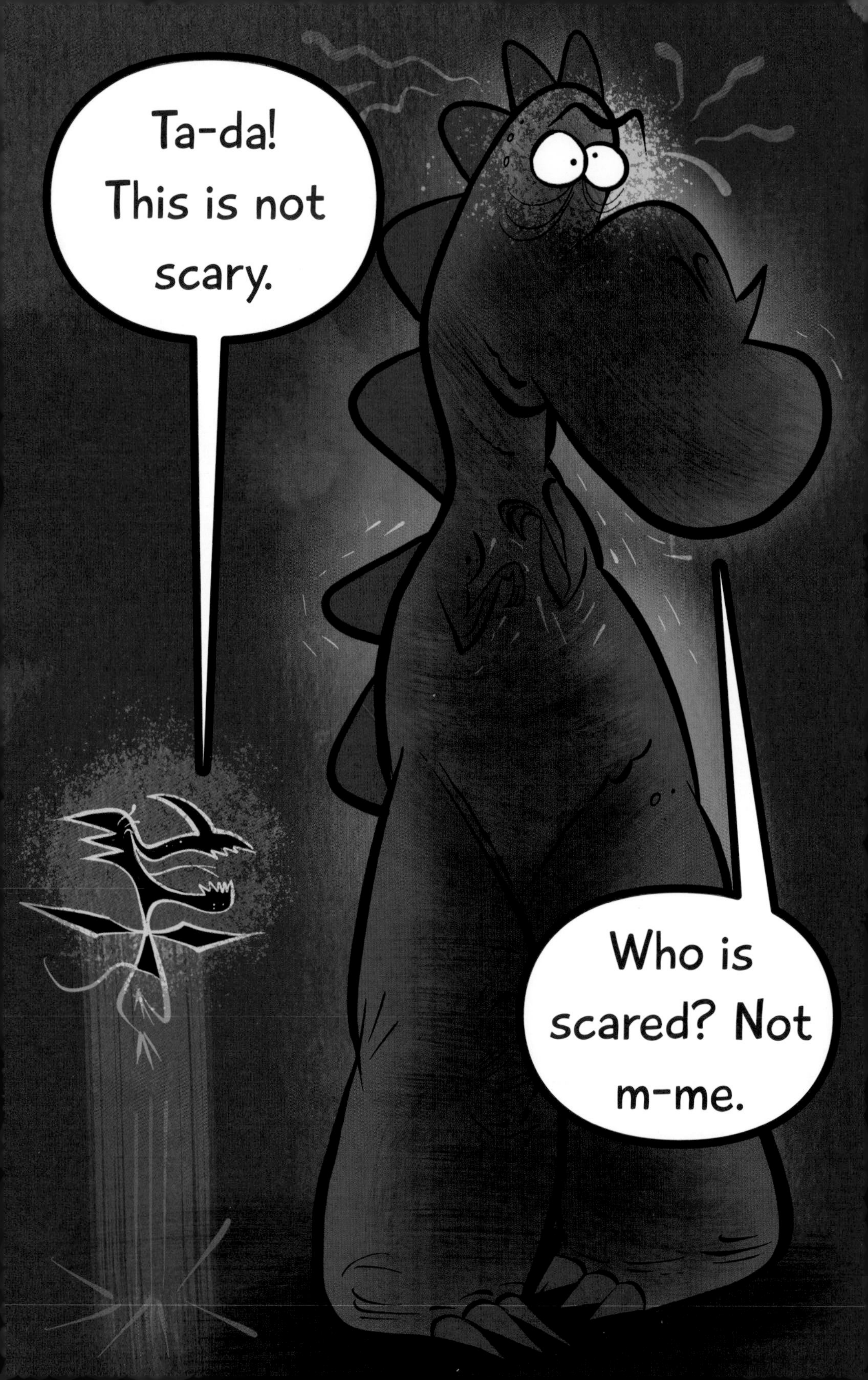
Ta-da! This is not scary.
Who is scared? Not m-me.

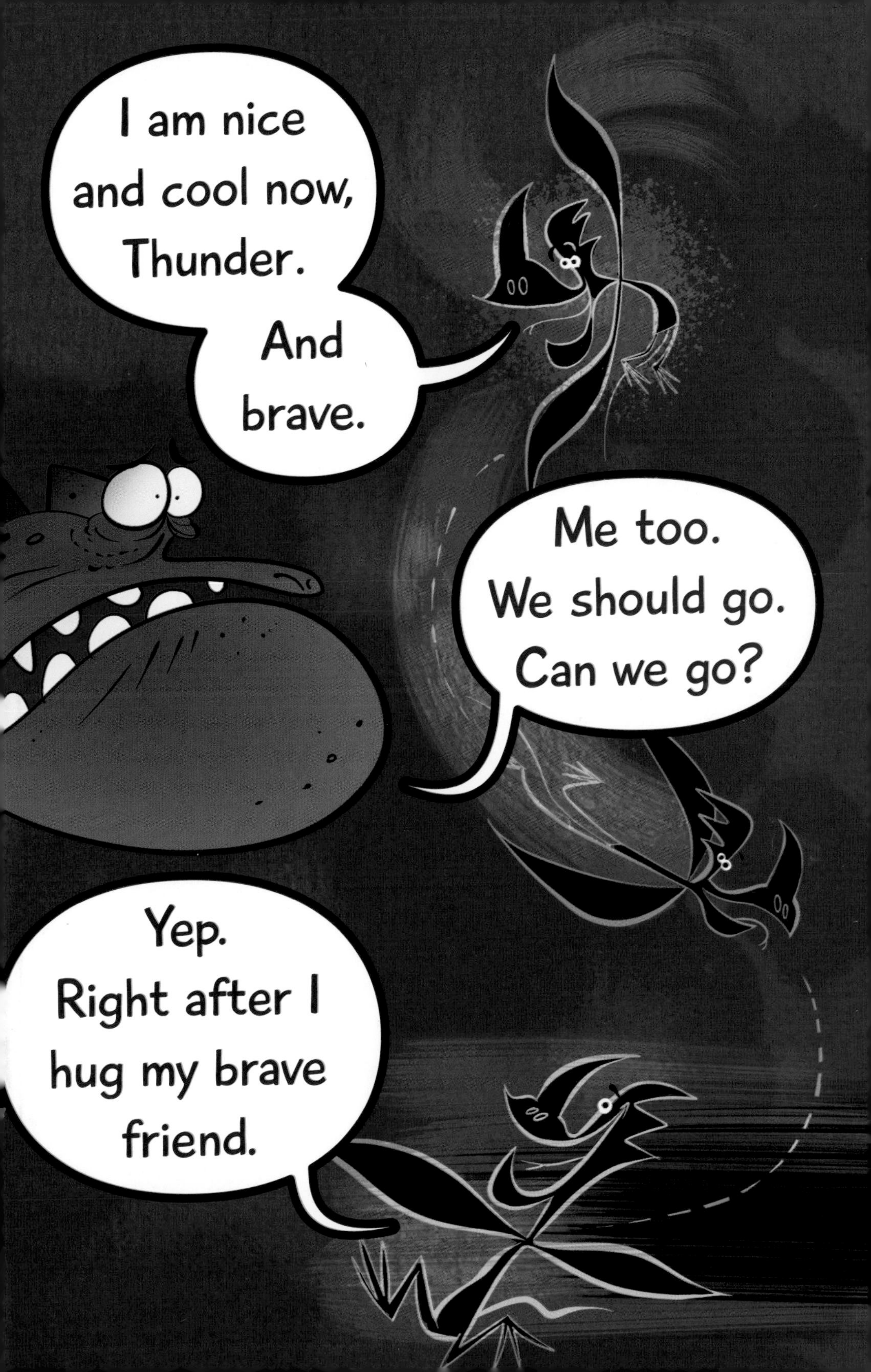
I am nice and cool now, Thunder.
And brave.
Me too. We should go. Can we go?
Yep. Right after I hug my brave friend.

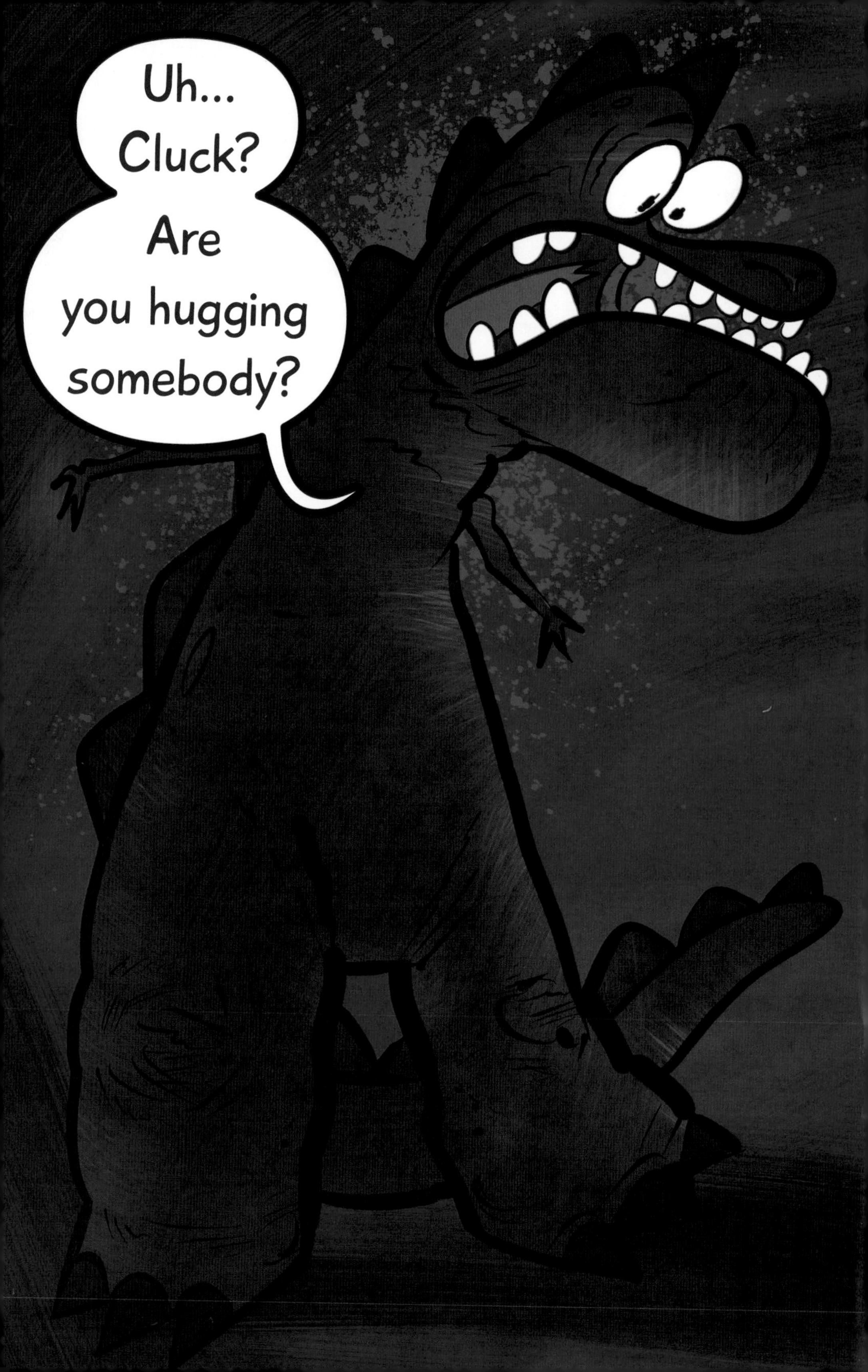
Uh... Cluck? Are you hugging somebody?

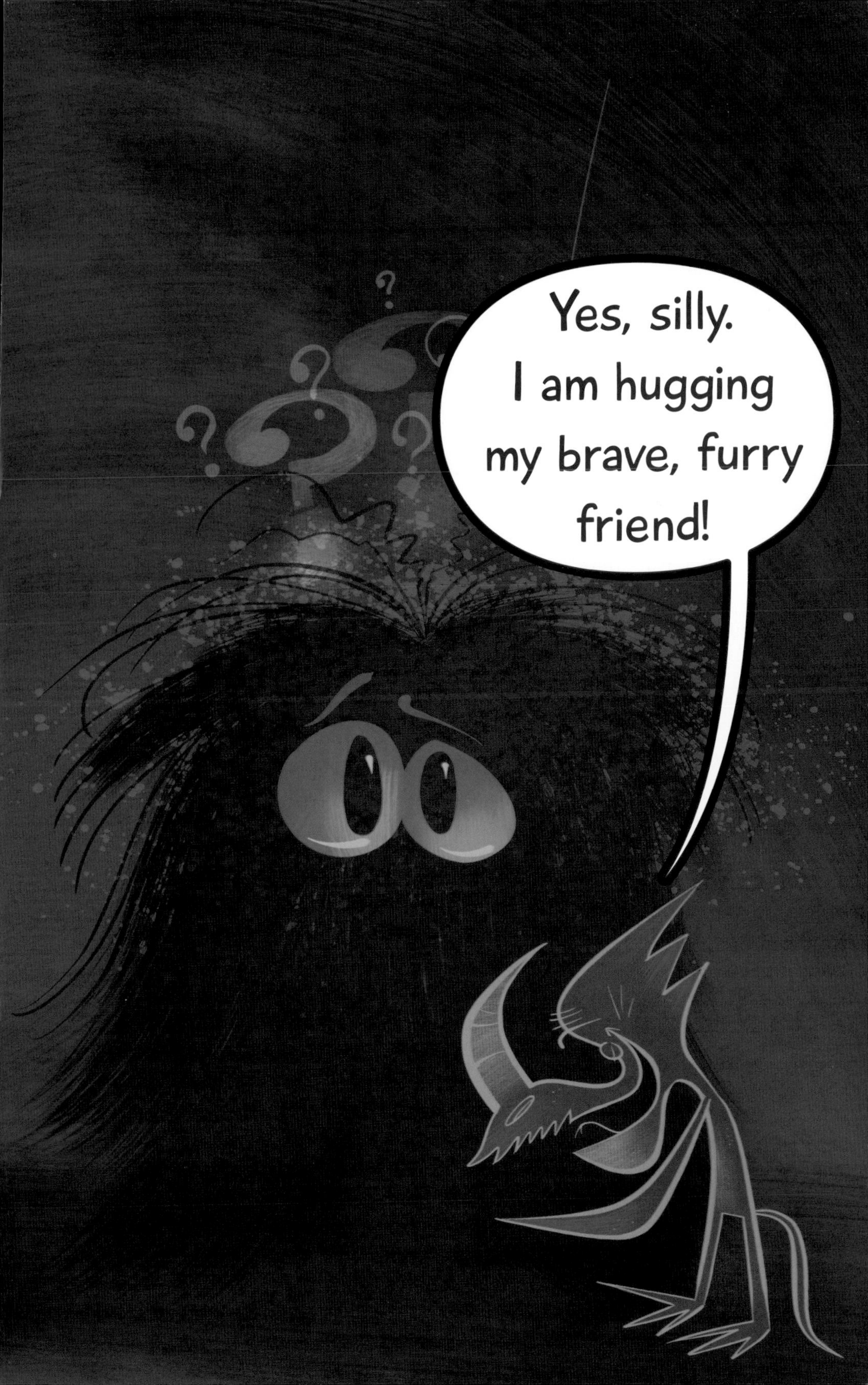
Yes, silly. I am hugging my brave, furry friend!

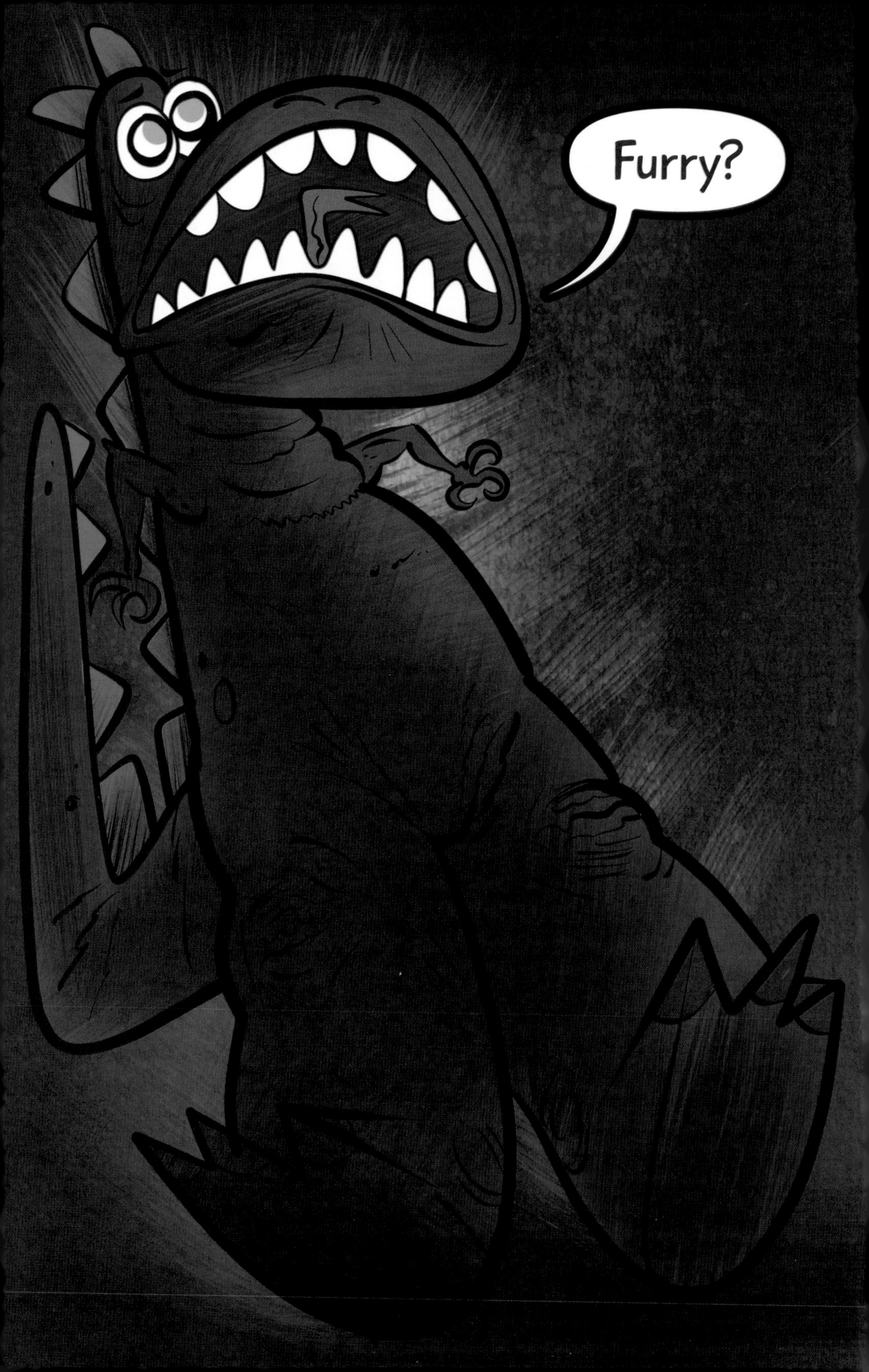
Furry?

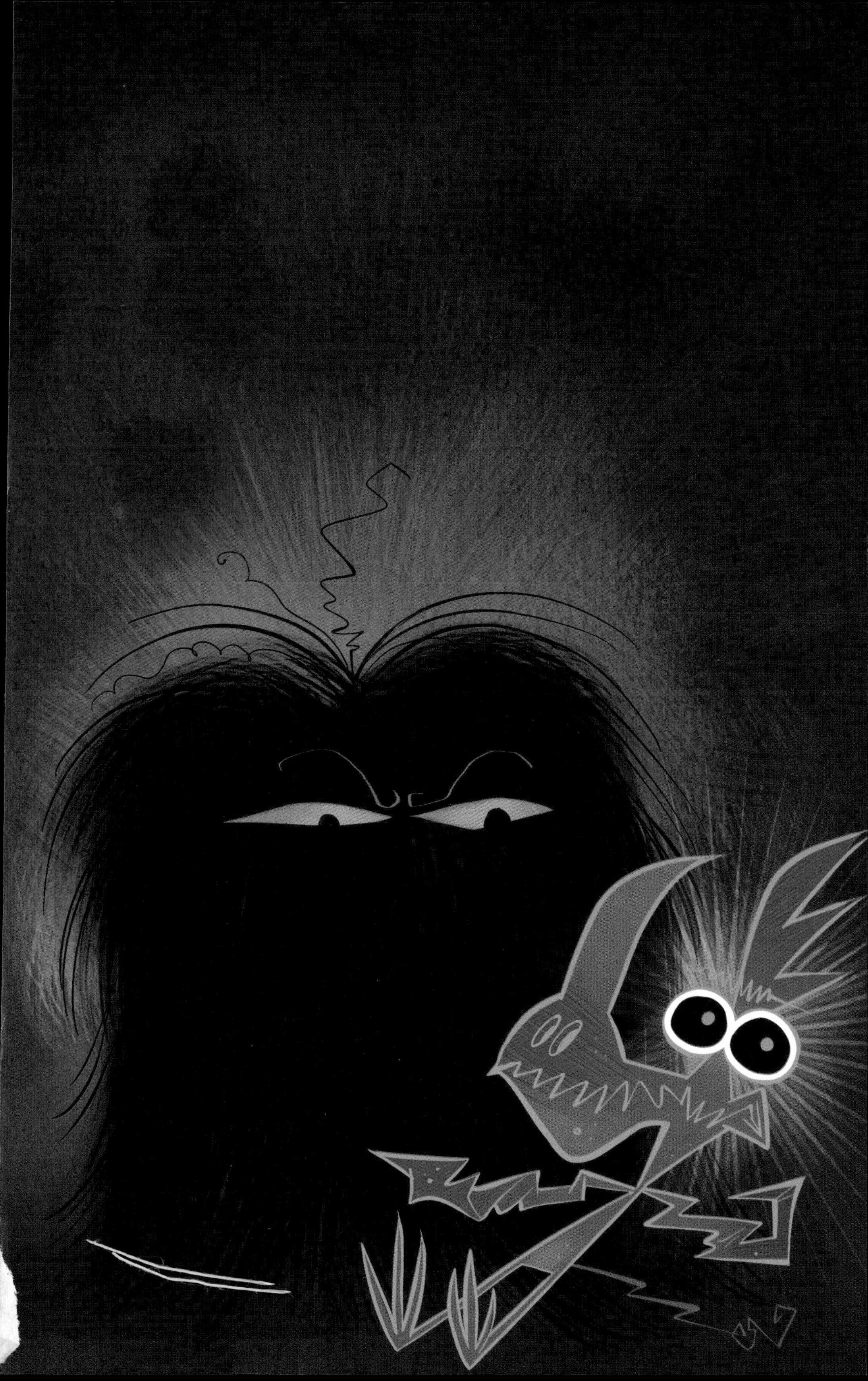

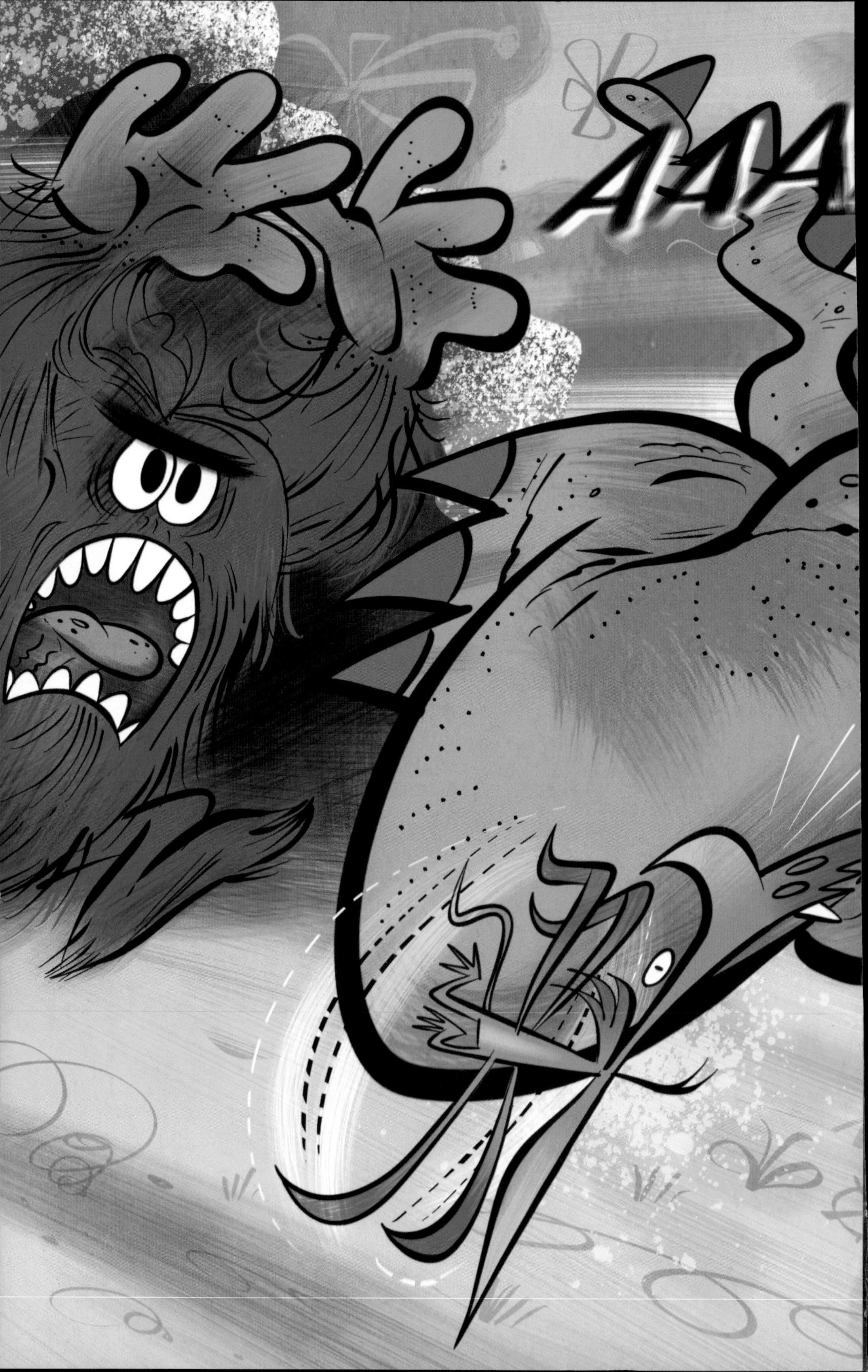
AAAA

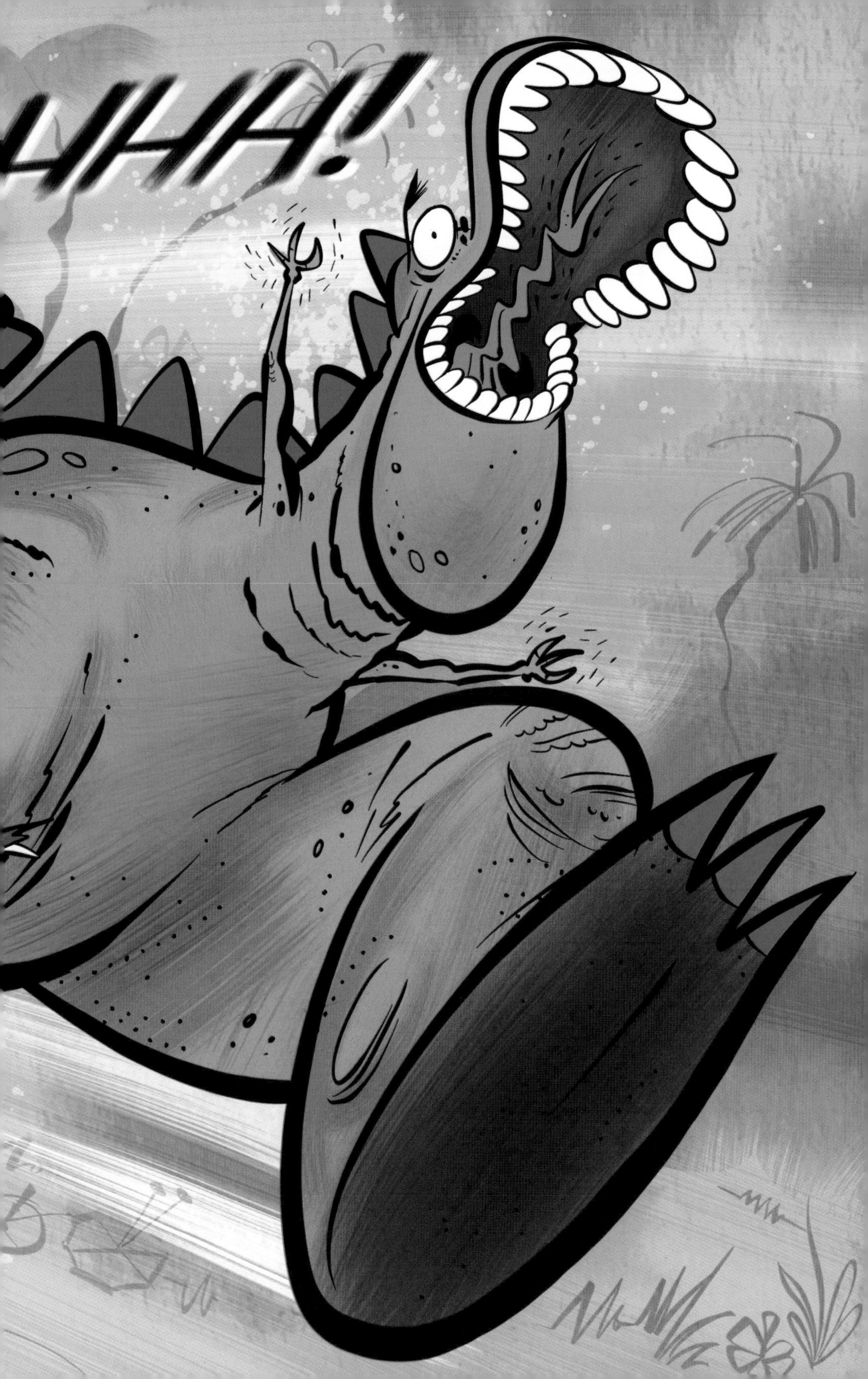
UHH!

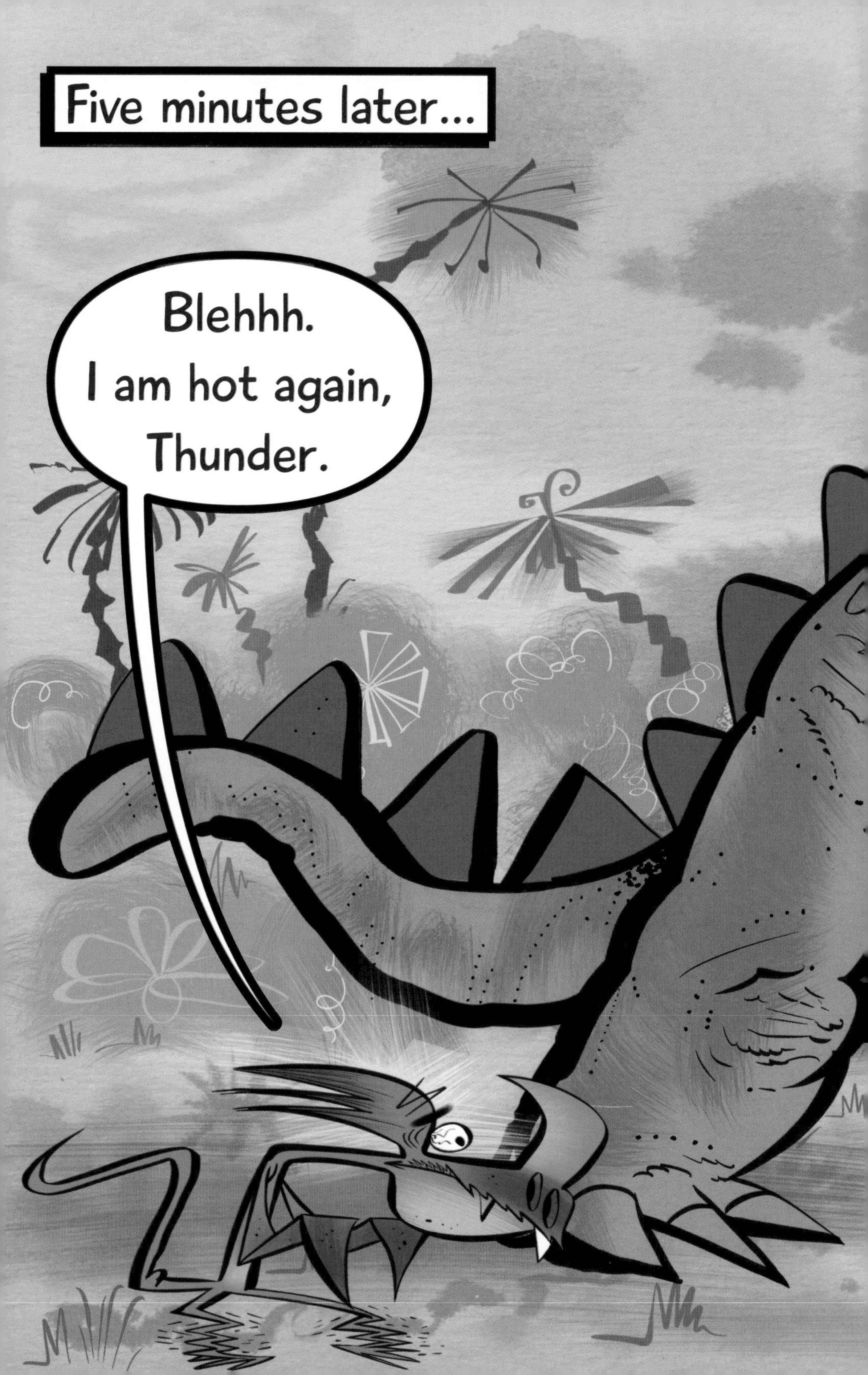
Five minutes later...
Blehhh.
I am hot again,
Thunder.

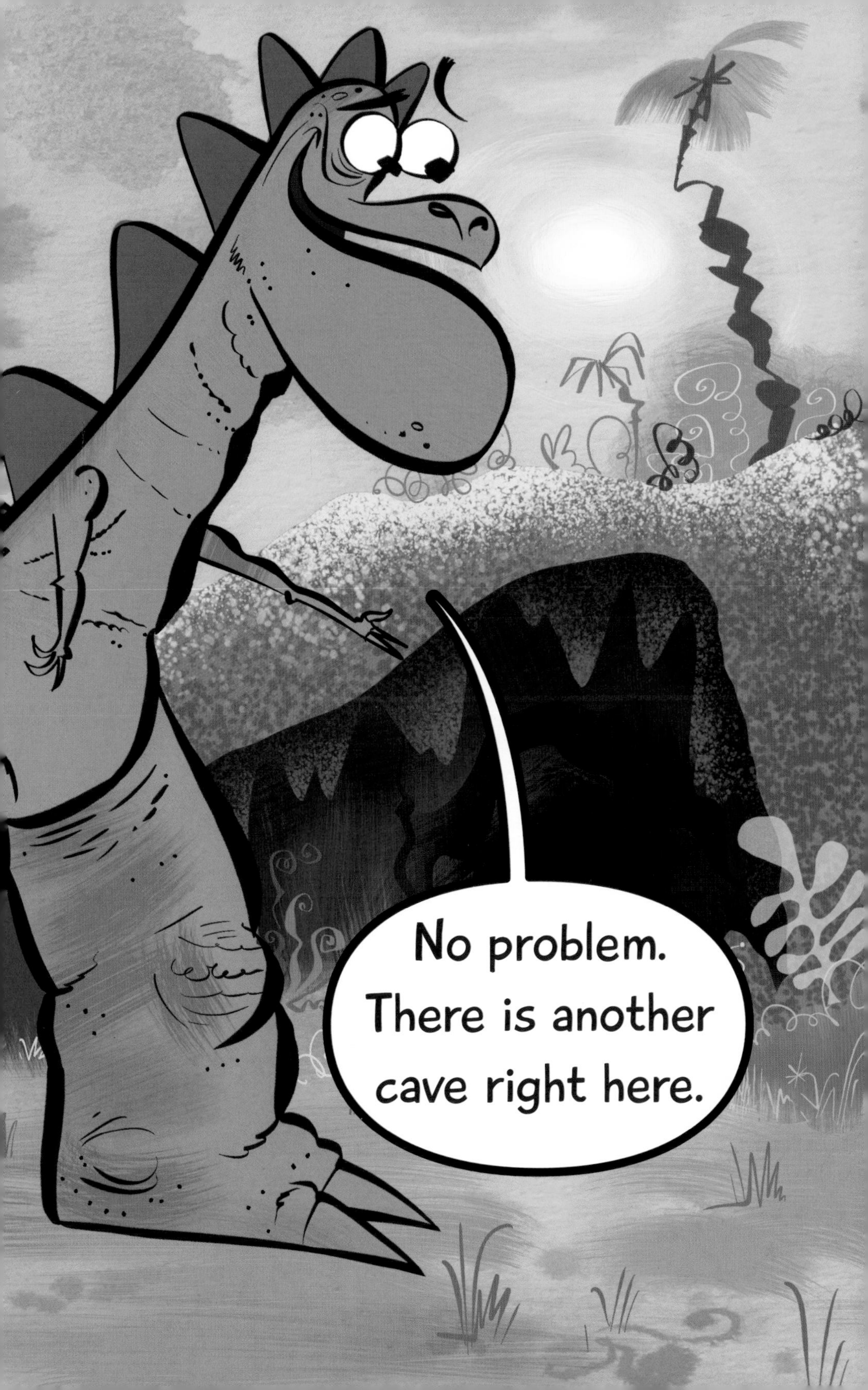
No problem. There is another cave right here.

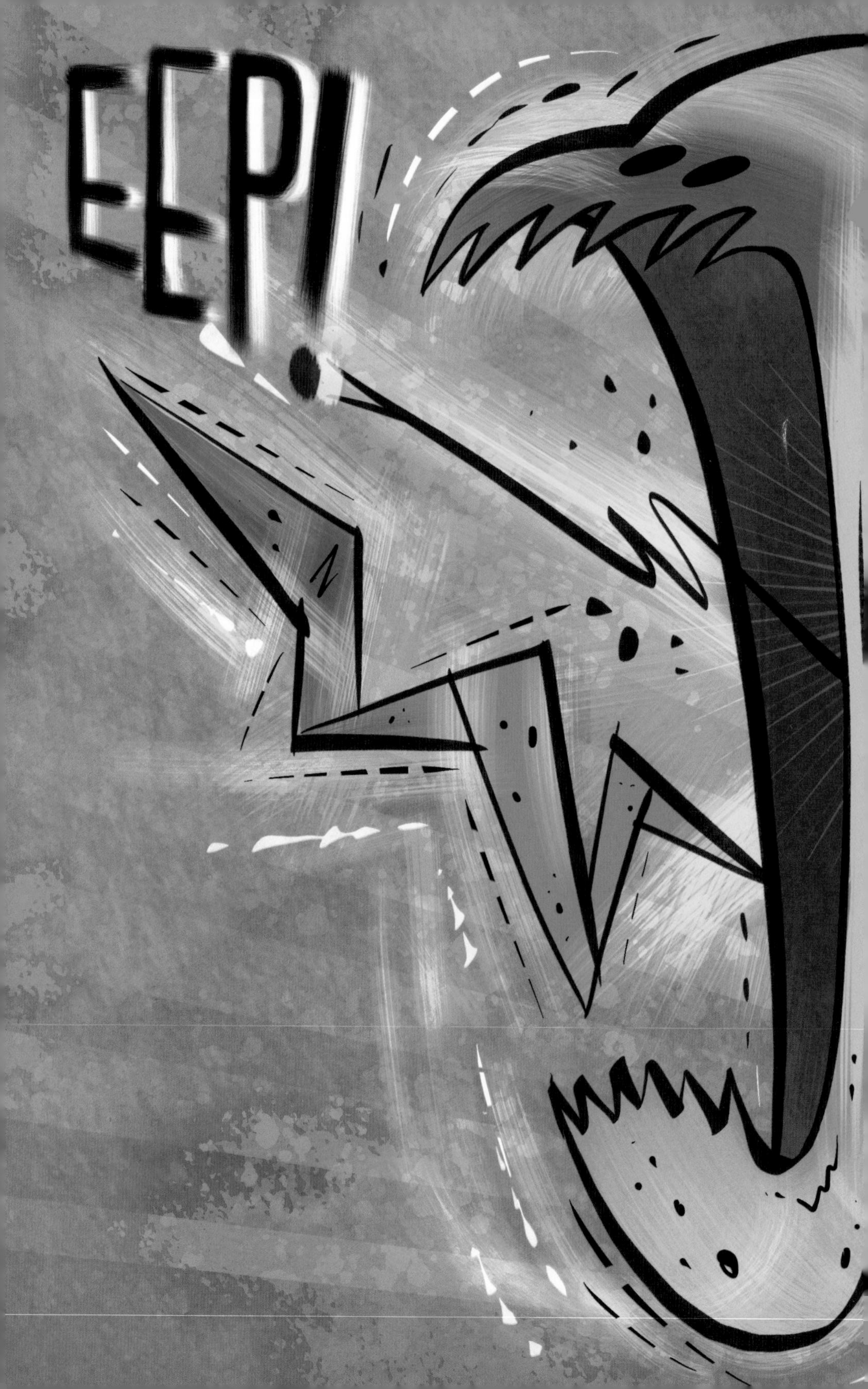
EEP!

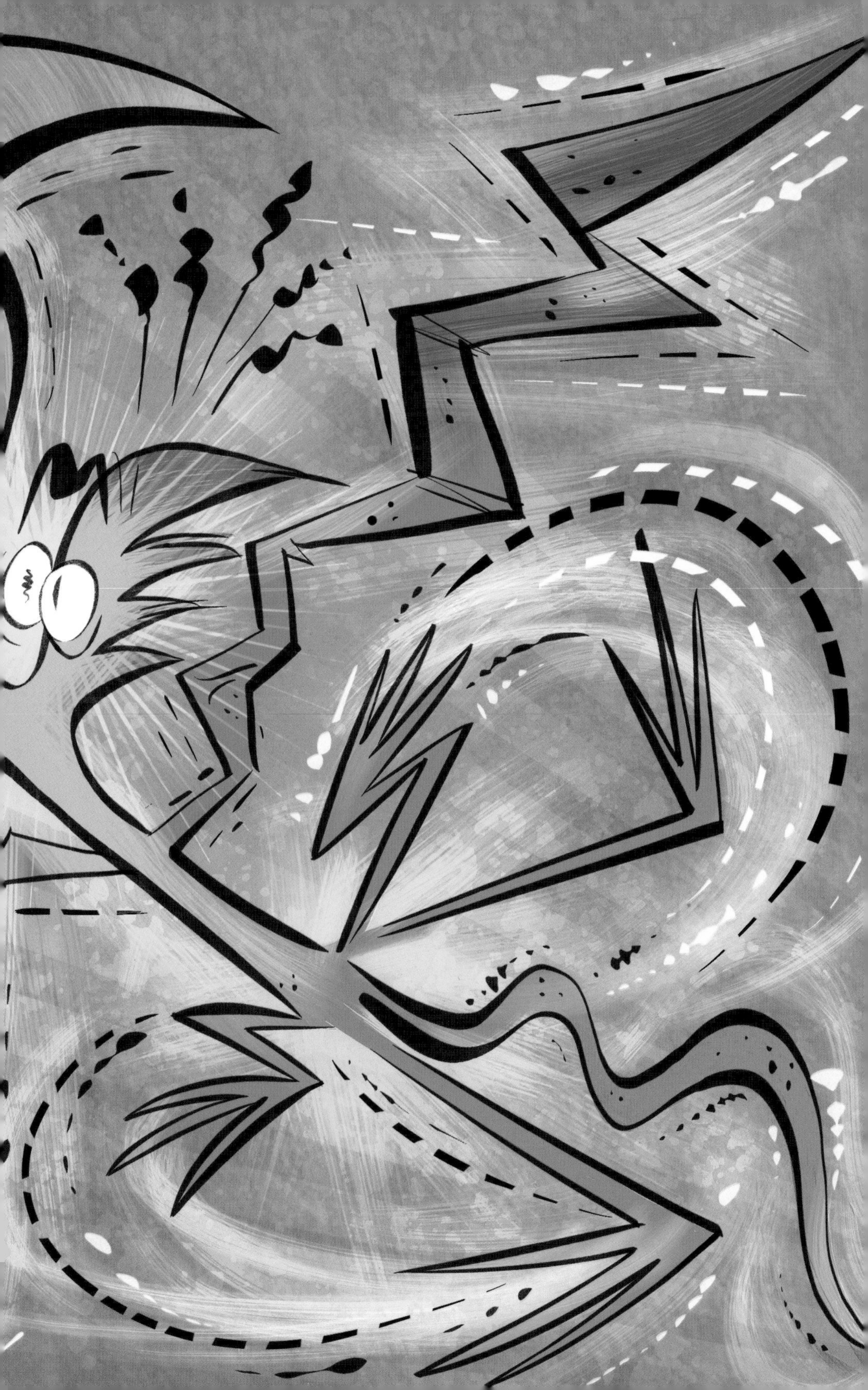

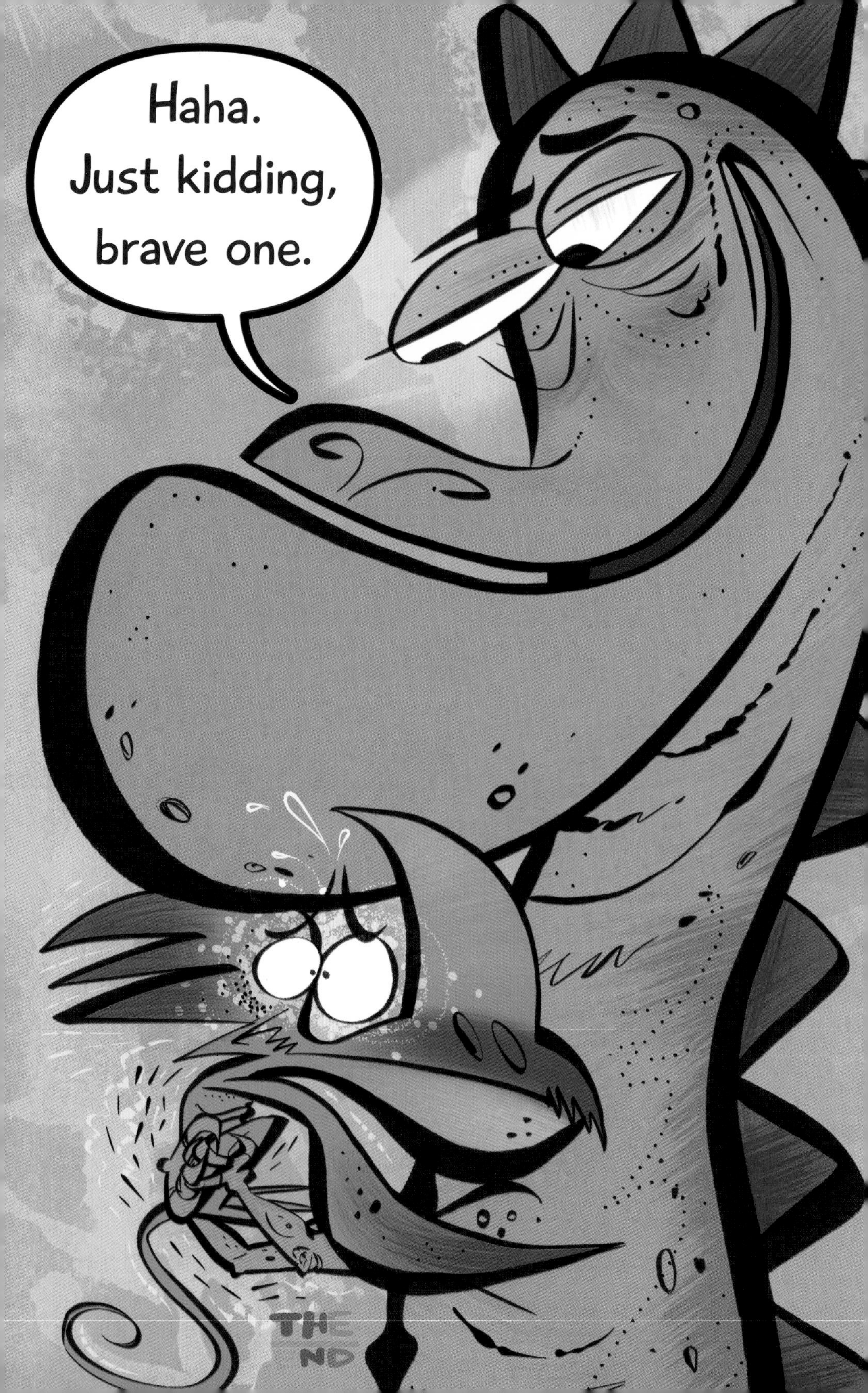
Haha. Just kidding, brave one.
THE END